THE WI
KING

Books by Mark Cheverton

The Gameknight999 Series
Invasion of the Overworld
Battle for the Nether
Confronting the Dragon

The Mystery of Herobrine Series: A Gameknight999 Adventure
Trouble in Zombie-town
The Jungle Temple Oracle
Last Stand on the Ocean Shore

Herobrine Reborn Series: A Gameknight999 Adventure
Saving Crafter
The Destruction of the Overworld
Gameknight999 vs. Herobrine

Herobrine's Revenge Series: A Gameknight999 Adventure
The Phantom Virus
Overworld in Flames
System Overload

The Birth of Herobrine: A Gameknight999 Adventure
The Great Zombie Invasion
Attack of the Shadow-Crafters
Herobrine's War

The Mystery of Entity303: A Gameknight999 Adventure
Terrors of the Forest
Monsters in the Mist
Mission to the Moon

The Gameknight999 Box Set
The Gameknight999 vs. Herobrine Box Set
The Gameknight999 Adventures Through Time Box Set

The Rise of the Warlords: A Far Lands Adventure
Zombies Attack!
The Bones of Doom
Into the Spiders' Lair

Wither War: A Far Lands Adventure
The Wither King
The Withers Awaken (Coming Soon!)
The Wither Invasion (Coming Soon!)

THE WITHER KING

WITHER WAR BOOK ONE: A FAR LANDS ADVENTURE

AN UNOFFICIAL MINECRAFTER'S ADVENTURE

MARK CHEVERTON

SKY PONY PRESS
NEW YORK

Copyright © 2018 by Mark Cheverton

Minecraft® is a registered trademark of Notch Development AB

The Minecraft game is copyright © Mojang AB

Sky Pony Press books may be purchased in bulk at special discounts
for sales promotion, corporate gifts, fund-raising, or educational
purposes. Special editions can also be created to specifications.
For details, contact the Special Sales Department, Sky Pony Press,
307 West 36th Street, 11th Floor, New York, NY 10018 or info@
skyhorsepublishing.com.

Sky Pony® is a registered trademark of Skyhorse Publishing, Inc.®,
a Delaware corporation.

Visit our website at www.skyponypress.com.

10 9 8 7 6 5 4 3 2 1

Library of Congress Cataloging-in-Publication Data is available on file.

Cover design by Brian Peterson
Cover artwork by Vilandas Sukutis (www.veloscraft.com)
Technical consultant: Gameknight999

Print Paperback ISBN: 978-1-51073-488-3
Ebook ISBN: 978-1-51073-491-3

Printed in the United States of America

ACKNOWLEDGMENTS

As always, I want to thank my family for their support and encouragement; they keep me motivated and challenge me to come up with new and better ideas. I'd like to thank the great people at Skyhorse Publishing. Their continued faith in my stories is heartwarming. Lastly, I'd like to thank Mrs. Holl and her fourth- and fifth-grade writers. Her dedication to her students is incredible. She's taught students the joy of writing and crafting stories and made writing cool in her elementary school. The excitement these young writers now have for the stories and characters they're creating is fantastic and invigorating. It is the highlight of my day to see the spark of creativity burning bright in their eyes. So, to all of Mrs. Holl's young writers, I say "Thank You!"

NOTE FROM THE AUTHOR

I'm so thrilled that so many readers have embraced Watcher and his companions. I've wanted to write about these characters and the Far Lands for a long time, and I'm really enjoying creating these stories for you. But the warm acceptance all of you have shown to these characters has been just incredible.

I've seen fan fiction written about Watcher and the wither king on numerous fan fiction sites. I've seen stories about Blaster and his joy of blowing things up, and of course, there are stories about Er-Lan, the zombie everyone loves, but fears just a little. I read and love all the stories that are sent to me; it's been fantastic to see what all of you can create with these characters.

If you've written your own story and you want to send it to me, send it through my website, www.mark-cheverton.com, but be sure to spell your email address correctly so that I can send you a link to your story. Please keep sending me your emails, through my website, letting me know what you think about my stories. I answer every email personally, so if you have questions or ideas for new stories, or you want to know about my background, or you want to see a hologram of me on youtube (https://youtu.be/vtf_-i9CXEo), or you want to know how fat my cat really is . . . then send me an email and ask; I answer every email!

Keep creating your stories, keep reading, and watch out for creepers.

Mark

What's inside you is always more important than what's on the outside. It's great to have the best clothing, newest smartphones, shiniest jewelry . . . but when that stuff is necessary for you to be accepted, then you're with the wrong people. Stuff and ego can become a mask, hiding the real you that's inside.

We're all afraid of rejection. We're all afraid of not being good enough. We're all the same. The trick is to realize this truth and just accept who you are. Be grateful for your strengths, work on your weaknesses, and be the real you who hides behind your mask.

CHAPTER 1

The Eternal Prison stood alone on the cold and lonely mountaintop.

Like the rest of the structure, the gleaming, razor-sharp iron spikes lining the obsidian wall were untouched by the ravages of time. Krael, king of the withers, smiled as he moved toward the fortified wall. The metal gates that had once barred his entrance now laid shattered and in pieces on the ground; he'd destroyed them after he found the first Crown of Skulls, the magic artifact that had given him the extra power necessary to breach the entrance.

The wither king's three heads smiled, the left and right skulls glancing at the one in the center with pride.

"Finally, we have returned," Center said, grinning. "It has been far too long."

"Now that we have the second Crown of Skulls, things will be different." Left glared at their surroundings, a look of malice in his dark eyes.

"Yes," Center agreed. The dark skull glanced at Left and smiled at the sight of the golden crown atop the ashen head; it was the same as the one Center wore. "With two Crowns of Skulls, each enchanted with magical power, our flaming skulls will be strong enough to release them."

"Why do we need the Broken Eight again?" Right always needed to see the logic in things.

Center scowled. He'd explained this to the other skulls many times already. "The magic infused into the Broken Eight will allow them to enter the Cave of Slumber. They will be the key to releasing our wither army."

"And Kora," Right added.

"Yes . . . Kora," Center murmured as he thought about their wife. It had been centuries since she had been captured with the other withers at the end of the Great War. "The Broken Eight will be instrumental in freeing Kora and the other withers."

"I knew that." Left sounded proud.

Center knew Left was not as smart as Right; all he wanted to do was fight. With a scowl levied at Left, Center continued. "It has been a long time. I miss her." The other two heads nodded. "Now, with the power of two Crowns, we may be strong enough to release the Eight . . . and Kora." A long-endured sadness filled his voice. All three skulls missed Kora, but Center longed for her the most.

"Then let's get going." Left's abrupt voice was jarring; he was never very sensitive to others' feelings.

Right thought Center would yell at Left, but instead, he just nodded, and the wither king floated through the hole in the barricade.

The fortress was, of course, empty. It had stood upon this mountaintop for centuries. After the Great War between the NPC wizards and monster warlocks, it was used to hold the most violent prisoners, all of whom, except for the Broken Eight, perished during their captivity. The magical enchantments used to create those ancient warriors had somehow given them extended lives.

Soon, the Eight will be free again, Krael thought.

They'll be able to do what they were created to do: destroy.

Gliding across a courtyard of snow-covered stone, the wither king glanced up at the many watchtowers looming high over the structure. These archer towers pointed inward, toward the courtyard and passage entrances, rather than outward to repel an attacking army. No army had ever assaulted this structure, for no one ever came to the Eternal Prison voluntarily. This was a place where hope came to die, and everyone feared it . . . except for Krael, the king of the withers.

The monster entered a shadowy passage he knew led to the cells in the deepest and darkest part of the prison. The magical enchantments embedded in the two golden crowns sitting upon two of his three heads cast an iridescent purple glow, giving him just enough light to see where he was going. Floating just off the ground, he followed the passage as it descended through the catacombs of the prison until it finally ended in a large, dungeon-like room. Cold stone bricks covered the walls and floors. At places on the walls, moss covered the bricks, but the enchantments woven into this place had gnawed at the velvety growth, slowly leaching its life away until it turned a sickly brown. Only the newest moss still held any green color, though it was already fading.

Krael floated into the terrible chamber and smiled. "I bet you didn't expect me to return," the wither king said to the ancient structure. "Now that I have two Crowns of Skulls. The enchantments of this ancient prison may not be strong enough to keep me from freeing my new friends."

Left laughed, making an awful hissing sound, as he glanced up at Center. Right gave the skull an angry glare, but Left ignored her.

"I'm sure the ancient wizards never expected any of the Broken Eight ever to be released," Right said, her voice soft and smooth, almost like a song.

"Why didn't the NPC (non-playable character) wizards just destroy these zombies?" Left asked, curious.

"When the monster warlocks created these ancient warriors, the enchantments used on them were so powerful, their foes, the wizards, lacked the power to destroy them with just magic alone. They tried, but were unsuccessful. Only the sharpest blade wielded by the greatest warrior had any hope of even scratching one of the Broken Eight." Center glanced at Left and Right, making sure they were listening. "But near the end of the Great War, even the warlocks found their creations had become difficult to control. That is why they are called the Broken Eight: the spells used to create them broke, releasing them from the control of their masters."

"Then how do you know we can control them?" Right asked, sounding suddenly worried.

"Because of the Crown of Skulls." Center gestured to his crown and the one on Left's head, grinning coldly. "These ancient relics will give us the power to control and destroy them."

"Their prison cells are down the next corridor," Left said.

The creature moved into the passage. Torches, burned out long ago, sat on the walls, their sooty ends blackened with ash. As Krael floated forward, his broad shoulders knocked many of the cold torches to the ground, where the wood instantly crumbled to splinters; the centuries had not been kind. With his way still lit by the magical power leaking from the Crown of Skulls, Krael floated through the corridor, a circle of iridescent light bathing the walls and floor. The tunnel finally ended at a large chamber lined with stone bricks, the floor covered by a thin layer of snow, undisturbed for hundreds of years.

"I am back, my friends." Krael's voice boomed, echoing off the ageless walls.

"We told you we would return," Right added. "And here we are."

Left just snarled.

The dark creature floated through the massive structure, looking around. A series of jail cells, barred with iron, lined the walls. A reflecting pool occupied the center of the chamber, with a column of netherrack standing three blocks high jutting out of the water. Flames licked the top of the column from the rusty, speckled cube of netherrack, forever burning and throwing bits of ash and smoke into the air. The flames kept the water from freezing in the frigid jail, but could not keep the moist spray from covering the ground with a thin, icy sheen.

As he passed the pool, Krael glanced down at his reflection. His skeletal body was black as soot, and bony ribs extended from his exposed spine, their dark texture making it look as if he'd just come out of a blast furnace. Three skulls sat atop his broad shoulders, the center and left heads each wearing a Crown of Skulls, the golden artifacts adorned with tiny black skulls spaced around their tops.

Within the prison cells were eight zombies, each accompanied by a huge wolf. The monsters wore golden armor that sparkled with magical enchantments, and each of their helms resembled a different ferocious creature. Their arms and chests bulged with muscles, as if their metallic armor was barely able to contain all their strength. Many of the creatures drew their swords as the wither entered the room, and the wolves began growling, their eyes turning bright red.

"Is the wither here to release us?" The tallest of the zombies asked, staring through the iron bars at his visitor. His helmet was in the shape of a dragon's head, and his eyes peered out of the golden, sharp-toothed mouth. "Or perhaps just here to gloat and mock?"

"Be patient, zombie," Krael's left skull snapped.

"This 'zombie' is named Ya-Sik, captain of the Broken Eight," the monster replied. "The Eight have been imprisoned in these cells since the Great Wars.

For hundreds of years, patience has been the only thing available . . . patience and a thirst for revenge."

"Well, perhaps it is time for that revenge," Center said.

The other seven zombies immediately sprang to their feet. Each wore identical, golden armor, with rare gems studding the chest plates and shoulders, their helmets resembling a different kind of monster. The golden metal of their gem-studded armor glowed, like the Crown of Skulls, as magical enchantments pulsed through the metallic coatings, causing them to sparkle with mysterious power.

Ya-Sik removed his golden helmet and stared up questioningly at the king of the withers. "The last time Krael was here, it wasn't possible to open these cells." The zombie leader pointed at the left head with a razor-sharp claw. "That one mocked the Eight. Is that the wither king's purpose again?"

"No, my zombie. Things are very different from the last time we were here." Krael moved closer. "Notice, we now have two Crowns of Skulls. That gives us much greater power. Now, we can do things that were not possible last time we were here."

"Like what?" Ya-Sik was suspicious.

"Like, possibly releasing you and the rest of the Eight." Right's voice was soft and non-threatening.

"If we feel like it," Left screeched with a cruel smile.

"Left, be quiet." Center scowled at Left, then brought its lifeless gaze back to the Broken Eight in their cells.

"Is this true?" A zombie with a helmet shaped like a ghast moved to the bars.

"We will soon see, but you must understand something first." Krael slowly turned in a circle, focusing his cold stare on each of the Eight. "If I can release the Broken Eight, then you will be mine to command."

The king of the withers glared at Ya-Sik. "Is that clear?"

The zombie glanced at his imprisoned comrades;

they all nodded in return. "The Broken Eight agree, as long as revenge against the wizards and villagers is possible." The zombie captain stared up at the wither king, their eyes locked in a test of wills. Krael smiled evilly.

"Revenge against the NPCs is exactly what I have in mind. And as far as I know, there's only one wizard alive. He may be just a boy, but I plan on destroying him with you and your comrades' help. We will not let the boy-wizard ever become a man."

The zombie gave Krael a crooked, toothy grin. "These zombies will happily destroy this wizard and any others brave enough to stand against the Broken Eight." The captain glanced at his zombie companions. They nodded their agreement.

The wolves sensed the zombies' excitement and howled ferociously.

"Our direwolves agree as well." Ya-Sik patted the furry-white animal at his side. "They, too, thirst for revenge."

Krael gave the zombie leader a nod, then floated to a nearby wall, where a switch sat on a pedestal of stone, a purple field of energy surrounding it. The wither king floated high in the air, staring at the glowing object. Last time they were here, he'd tried to move the lever, but the magical enchantment protecting the device had been too strong for Krael to surpass. But now, things were different . . . he hoped.

The Crown of Skulls atop the left head began to shine, giving off a purple radiance. The center Crown glowed as well, both of the magical artifacts becoming brighter and brighter. The harsh glare soon forced the zombies to look away as the light's intensity became too great.

Suddenly, Krael fired a stream of flaming skulls at the switch. Each skull, wreathed in a coating of blue-black flames, sparkled with magic as it slammed into the enchanted lever. The skulls exploded on impact, filling the chamber with thunderous crashes. The wither king kept firing, blasting the lever with skull projectiles, using every last drop of his power and strength. The glowing field around the switch grew smaller and smaller as the flaming skulls battered the protective enchantment, until finally . . . it flickered and disappeared.

Quickly, Krael fired one more skull, which struck the lever and pushed it to the side until it clicked into place. Instantly, lines of redstone powder on the cold floor came to life, melting through the thin layer of snow and ice covering them. The glowing signal moved to each jail cell door, allowing the iron doors to swing outward. The shimmering layers of magic surrounding each cell flickered as the doors swung open.

"Now . . . get out of the cells!" Krael shouted.

The eight zombies each leaped out of their cells, followed by their direwolves. In a blink of an eye, the magical spells wrapped around each jail cell burst back into life and the iron doors slammed shut as the enchantments regained their vitality . . . but it was too late.

The Broken Eight were free.

"It is time for revenge," Ya-Sik growled. The other zombies nodded, drawing their golden short swords and pulling their golden shields from their inventories. The shields were curved, letting them wrap around the wielders' bodies, and their fronts were covered with razor-sharp barbs. The zombie warriors were a terrifying sight to behold, and Krael loved it.

"Absolutely." Krael's three heads nodded. "And at the top of the list is a certain boy-wizard I know. He's meddled in my plans one too many times, and now, at last, it's time for his destruction." He glanced at the zombies and smiled. "I can't wait for that puny wizard to meet my new friends . . . the Broken Eight."

The zombies clanked their golden swords against their spiked shields while the huge direwolves howled with angry delight.

The king of the withers laughed as he floated across the floor and out of the ancient structure, eight vicious zombie warriors following close behind.

CHAPTER 2

Watcher moved through the passage under the Wizard's Tower, his nerves feeling like old bowstrings stretched to their limits. Shadows covered the walls of the corridor, his imagination putting terrifying beasts in the darkness, ready to attack. A sparkling circle of purple light surrounded him and his friends, coming partially from his enchanted sword, Needle, which he held at the ready. The magical power laced throughout the weapon cast a soft purple glow on the tunnel walls, but it was dwarfed by the light coming from the boy's arms. Holding them out, Watcher was still surprised when he saw them glowing, the sparkling light pulsing from his fingertips to his shoulders as if the magical enchantments moving through his body were somehow alive.

"You make a good torch," a voice said next to him. A smile emerged from the shadows, then moved closer, resolving into his friend, Blaster, in his favorite midnight-black leather armor. "You think there might still be monsters down here? We've searched the Wizard's Tower many times."

"I know, but we need to be sure." Watcher put away his sword and pulled out a torch. "I'm a little nervous about any surprises after moving everyone from our village into this place."

"You know we couldn't stay in the savannah," a soft and lyrical voice said from behind them.

Planter, his best friend—and new girlfriend—moved to his side and put a hand on his shoulder. It felt as if fireworks were going off in his heart. He smiled at her, forgetting about the fact they were hunting dangerous monsters.

"After defeating the spider warlord's army of monsters, we all knew it would be too dangerous to stay in the savannah; the monsters knew where we were." Planter moved her hand from his shoulder to his hand and interlaced her fingers with his. "Moving everyone to the Wizard's Tower was a great idea, Watcher." Her voice was soft and soothing.

Blaster coughed. "Umm . . . maybe we should focus on the job at hand?"

"Oh . . . ahh . . . yeah, of course." Watcher's cheeks grew hot; he hoped none of them would notice in the shadowy passage. Pulling his hand from Planter's, he put the torch in his left hand and drew Needle again.

"Watcher, why do you think there are more unexplored tunnels or rooms in the Wizard's Tower?" Blaster asked. "I've been through this structure a hundred times."

"I know, but since this happened," Watcher held out his glowing arms, "hidden doorways have been opening when I come near. I guess it's because of me."

"You mean because you're now this all-powerful wizard?" Blaster's question had a friendly, mocking tone.

"Well . . . I *am* a wizard, after all." Watcher glanced at his friend. "Your arms aren't glowing, are they?"

Blaster shook his head.

"Then it must be my new wizarding abilities that are opening up these things." Watcher stood a little taller, feeling empowered by the fact that he was a real, living wizard, the first since the long-ago Great War fought between the NPC wizards and monster warlocks.

Planter groaned.

Blaster sighed. "Not this again."

"I'm just saying, we've searched all these passages before and found nothing new. But now, we're finding brand new corridors that weren't here before." Watcher patted the stone wall with an outstretched hand. "It's like the walls are opening up just for me."

Blaster suddenly held up a hand. "You hear that?"

"No . . . what?" Watcher stared at the boy, curious.

"It was me rolling my eyes *so much*, I could hear them bouncing around in my sockets." Blaster laughed and patted his friend on the back. "Now get over yourself, and let's get this passage searched."

"I agree," Planter added, her voice sounding a little exasperated.

Watcher sighed. *They don't understand how hard it is to be a wizard. If they just—*

"Wait . . . I heard something." Planter leaned forward, cupping her hand around her ear.

Watcher sighed, expecting another joke. He was accustomed to being made fun of; it had been the favorite pastime of bullies when he was younger. "I don't think we have time for—"

"Shhh . . . a humming sound." Planter held a hand up, silencing him. "Follow me."

They moved slowly through the passage, the glow from Watcher's arms revealing the stone walls and floors around them, but doing little to shine any light on the rest of the tunnel. They went maybe twenty-five blocks until Planter stopped and pointed at the ground.

"Right here, the humming is coming from right here." She pointed at the block beneath her feet. "There's something under these bricks."

Watcher glanced doubtfully at Blaster; they both had expressions of uncertainty on their faces.

"Dig it up," Planter said.

It sounded like a command, and neither dared

refuse. Blaster pulled out an iron pickaxe as Planter stepped aside. After three hits, the stone bricks shattered, revealing a dusty wooden chest.

With a satisfied smile, Planter knelt and opened the chest. Inside the ancient box was just a single item: a necklace, glowing with magical power. She reached in and pulled it from the chest, then closed the lid. With her holding the amulet in the air, Watcher was able to get a good look at it.

The necklace was made from the finest silver chain, almost too thin to see without moving very close. At the end of the necklace was a shiny square of metal that was perfectly reflective, almost mirrorlike in its appearance, like the surface of Watcher's sword, Needle. At the center of the metallic square was a blood-red gem that glowed as if powered from within; it reminded Watcher of the eye of a spider. The chain and reflective square pulsed with magical power.

"You better let me have that; it's magic. I can handle it." Watcher reached out for the amulet, but Planter pulled it back.

At that moment, it flashed with power, the gemstone glowing a bright red, and Planter put her hands to her ears as if some loud noise had just blasted through the passage.

"Did you two hear that?" she asked.

Watcher and Blaster both shook their heads.

"It said 'Amulet of Planes,' but it sounded as if someone yelled it from inside my mind." She looked scared. "What's that mean?"

"I don't know, but maybe you should just put it in your inventory for now." Watcher knelt and replaced the stone bricks back on top of the chest. "Maybe Mapper will know what it is. We'll show it to him later."

Then the scuff of a boot across the stone floor echoed off the ancient walls, barely audible.

"Shhh." Watcher held a glowing hand up to stop his friends.

"What? Did the wizard detect a disturbance in the Far Lands?" Blaster chuckled.

"Be quiet . . . something's following us." Watcher put away the torch and reached into his inventory for his bow. His fingers brushed across the Fossil Bow of Destruction, the ancient relic he'd taken from the skeleton warlord many months ago. Watcher pulled the Bow out and grabbed the string.

Every time he touched it, he was nervous. The ancient weapon was reported to only be usable by wizards; any non-magic person using this weapon would be killed by its powerful magical enchantments. He was always cautious when using the Bow.

As soon as Watcher drew the string back, a sparkling arrow appeared, its sharp tip glinting with magical power. Pain surged through him as the ancient weapon dug into his health points (HP), using his body as a source of energy for the enchantments woven into the relic. Watcher gasped, always shocked at how much it hurt, but he remained motionless nonetheless; who knew what might emerge from the shadows?

Blaster drew his two curved knives and disappeared into the darkness, moving noiselessly through the passage, trying to sneak behind their potential assailant.

Planter pulled out her enchanted shield, a bright red rectangle with three black skulls emblazoned across the surface, its light adding to the shimmering glow around them. She held her enchanted golden axe in her right hand, ready for battle, her beautiful blond hair almost sparkling in the iridescent light.

"I know you're out there," Watcher's loud voice echoed off the cold stone walls. He placed a torch on the ground, then backed away, pulling Planter with him. "Step into the light, and I won't open fire."

Pain exploded through his body again as the Fossil Bow of Destruction stabbed at his health, drawing more energy into the ancient weapon. Watcher grunted as the waves of agony crashed through him but stayed on his feet.

A wizard wouldn't fall, he thought, the pain growing steadily.

"Umm," a high-pitched voice said. "It's only me."

A young girl stepped into the torchlight. She wore a tan smock with a black stripe running down the center. Her long blond hair, tied in a ponytail, hung over her shoulder, stretching down almost to her waist; it was Fencer.

Watcher gave an exasperated groan and lowered the bow, grateful to put it back into his inventory, stopping the pain.

"What are you doing here?" Planter was angry, her voice no longer soft and lyrical, but sharp as a knife.

"Well . . . I saw Watcher going into the darker parts of the building, and I wanted to make sure he was okay." Fencer glanced up at Watcher. The young girl's face lit up when she made eye contact with him.

Planter's body tensed as her rage built. Watcher knew she was getting ready to yell at the girl, and he didn't want that. Placing a hand on his girlfriend's shoulder, he stayed her anger, then took a step toward Fencer.

"I've told you before; you can't just follow me around." Watcher bent over and picked up the torch, then pulled out a loaf of bread and ate, allowing his HP to begin regenerating. As he neared, Fencer's smile grew bigger.

"I just wanted to make sure you didn't need anything." Fencer took a step toward Watcher.

"Like what?" Planter moved to Watcher's side. "We're here, searching for monsters or hidden traps. What did you think we needed? More weapons? More arrows? Did you bring any of those?"

"Well . . ." Fencer just shrugged, then looked away from Planter and toward Watcher again. A smile instantly grew on her face.

"Watcher, you're the bravest, most important person in all of Minecraft." She smiled a huge, joyous smile. "I'm gonna take care of you . . . forever."

Planter scowled at the young girl, her unibrow creased with annoyance.

"It's okay, Planter; she was just trying to help." Watcher gave Planter a quick smile. "I'm sure she was worried about all of us, weren't you, Fencer?"

The young girl just shrugged. She glanced at Planter and saw the angry glare levied toward her, then cast her gaze to the ground.

Planter moved her glare from Fencer to Watcher. "Watcher, sometimes, you're such an idiot."

"What?" He wasn't sure what she meant. "What did I do? I was just—"

Watcher stopped in mid-sentence and groaned. A sensation, not quite pain, but something similar, washed over his body, and he fell to one knee as the sound of multiple explosions echoed in his mind, mixed with a harsh, maniacal laughing.

"Watcher, what's wrong?" Planter caught him as he started to fall.

Another wave of discomfort smashed into his mind, filling him with a feeling that could only be described as spikey and evil. It drove the strength from his body, causing the magical purple glow woven through his arms to sputter and flicker.

The last of his strength faded, and his legs buckled. Planter held him in her arms and slowly settled him to the ground. "Watcher . . . what's wrong?" Planter pulled his diamond chest plate off his shoulders, making it easier for him to breathe.

Blaster stepped out of the darkness and stood protectively near Watcher and Planter, his eyes searching the shadows for enemies. Fencer pushed past the boy and knelt at Watcher's side, stroking his reddish-brown hair.

"It's okay, Watcher . . . it's okay." The young girl tried to hold Watcher's hand, but Planter shoved aside her grasp.

"Just leave him be," Planter snapped. She glared at

the girl, then looked down at her ill boyfriend. "Watcher . . . what's happening?"

"The Flail . . . I need the Flail." Watcher's voice was weak.

He reached into his inventory and curled his fingers around the leather-wrapped handle of the magical weapon. When he pulled it out, the Flail of Regret filled the passage with a pulsing glow. Magical power flowed from the spiked ball down the links of iron chain and into the wooden handle, throbbing and beating as if it were alive. Some of the power leaked into Watcher, reviving the iridescent energy wrapped around the boy's arms.

Instantly, a deep voice whispered in the back of his mind, pushing back on the waves of evil washing up against his brain. Watcher had learned there was some kind of living . . . thing . . . trapped within the magical weapon, and he could communicate with it.

The Broken Eight . . . the Broken Eight, the Flail said, its voice, for the first time, sounding terrified.

"The Broken Eight?" Watcher murmured, struggling to understand.

"What did you say?" Planter asked.

Watcher groaned.

Use the Eye . . . the Eye of Searching. The voice from the Flail sounded insistent.

With his other hand, Watcher reached into his inventory and found two long leather straps attached to a gold-rimmed glass lens: the magical artifact, the Eye of Searching. He'd taken it from the spider warlord when they defeated her, and now it was part of his magical arsenal. Pulling it from his inventory, he extended it to Planter.

"Blaster, get some healing potions ready." Watcher glanced at Planter. "Put it on me."

"You're too weak," she complained.

"Do it . . . please. It must be done."

With a sigh, Planter positioned the glass lens over

his eye, then tied the leather straps together at the back of his square head.

Instantly, pain stabbed into Watcher as the magical enchantment in the Eye of Searching looked for energy and found it within his HP. Almost at the same time, a glass bottle shattered against his chest, and cool liquid splashed across his body, quenching the flames of agony surging through him; it was the healing potion.

Concentrate on your enemy. The voice from the Flail of Regret sounded insistent.

Watcher had experimented with this artifact before and knew what it did: it would show an image of anyone or anything he imagined, but in real time, as if he were spying on them from some hidden perch. Closing his eyes, Watcher concentrated on his enemy, Krael, the king of the withers. Instantly, an image of the terrifying monster appeared in his mind.

The wither king floated down a snowy mountainside in the vision, wearing two Crowns of Skulls glowing with magical power. At first, it seemed to be a relatively insignificant scene, but then another monster stepped out from behind a frozen mound.

It was a zombie clad in magical, golden armor. The creature held a short sword in one hand and a curved shield in the other, and wore a dragon-shaped helmet over his scarred face. With a snarl, the zombie motioned for others to follow, and seven more gold-clad zombies stepped out from behind the snow-covered hill, each adorned in the same magical armor, each wearing a different-shaped monster-helmet. An evil energy seemed to emanate from the monsters, their enchanted boots leaving charred footprints on the ground. Behind the zombies came a pack of huge wolves, each of the animals almost the size of a small cow.

Direwolves. The voice from the Flail of Regrets was scared.

"Who are they?" Watcher asked, shaking with fear, the evil sensation from the zombies stabbing at his soul.

"What are you talking about?" Planter asked. She put a hand on Watcher's forehead, checking him for a fever, but he brushed it aside and concentrated on the vision.

Pain exploded again throughout his body, the price required by the Eye of Searching for the mystical view.

The eight zombies followed the wither king down the slopes, heading for a village at the foot of the mountain. Watcher knew they were going to destroy the community, not because they *had* to, but because they *wanted* to.

"No . . . don't do it!" Watcher shouted. He tried to stand, but he was too weak.

Just then, the wither king turned its center head and gazed into the sky. It felt as if the monster was staring right into Watcher's eyes. The terrifying creature laughed.

Behold your doom, the wither king said to Watcher with a smile, then looked away, as if dismissing him.

"Noooo . . ." Watcher cried out helplessly.

"It's okay, Watcher. You're here with us in the Wizard's Tower." Planter held him tight.

"Yeah . . . it's okay," Fencer said. She reached out and took Watcher's hand. "I'm here."

Planter glared at her.

Watcher shook his head as he watched the destruction of the village and its helpless inhabitants. The zombie warriors moved through the community like a storm of steel, slashing at anyone who moved or dared to resist; they were unstoppable. Some of the gigantic wolves darted between the buildings, destroying anyone who tried to flee, while others formed a bristling circle of fangs around the community, stopping anyone from running away. When the eight zombies finished their destructive deed, the wither king floated high into the air and bombarded the village with flaming skulls until every structure in the village was blasted into splinters, leaving nothing to show the community had ever existed except a charred stain on the surface of the Far Lands.

Reaching up, Watcher pulled the Eye of Searching from his head and dropped it to the ground. Instantly, the image disappeared from his mind and the pain from the enchanted relic dissipated. Blaster offered him a slice of melon, which he ate quickly, the food helping to restore his health.

"Are you okay?" Planter asked worriedly as she helped him to a sitting position.

"I can't believe it." Watcher shook, the horror of what he'd just witnessed still echoing in his mind. He looked down and found he still had the Flail of Regrets clutched in his right hand.

Did that really happen? the young wizard said in his mind, sending the thoughts to the magical weapon.

Yes, the weapon replied. *The wither has released the Broken Eight. What could not be released* has *been released. The world is in great peril.*

And then the voice grew quiet.

"Watcher . . . what happened?" Blaster helped the boy to his feet.

Fencer tried to grab an arm and help, but Blaster nudged her gently out of the way.

"The wither king has released some zombies that had been imprisoned . . . somewhere." Watcher glanced around at his friends with a worried expression. "Something bad is gonna happen, and Krael is at the center of it again. I have to talk to Mapper, right now."

"Come on, then." Fencer grabbed his arm. "I'll make sure you get back to the village okay."

Watcher nodded, then took off running with Fencer through the passage, leaving Planter and Blaster standing there.

Planter shook her head and gave an exasperated sigh.

"I heard that, Planter," Blaster said with a smile.

"Heard what? The sigh?"

"No, the other thing."

"What other thing?"

"Your eyes rolling." He put a reassuring hand on her shoulder, then followed Watcher and Fencer, Planter a few steps behind.

CHAPTER 3

Watcher moved through the dark passages with the destruction of the village playing over and over again in his mind; the cruel laughter from the wither king was a macabre soundtrack to the scene.

"I can't believe he just destroyed everyone." He shook his head, trying to dislodge the images, but they were permanently scorched into his mind.

"I'm sure you can take care of it, Watcher." Fencer's voice was a welcome distraction. "We'll make it to the others soon."

"Where are Planter and Blaster?" Watcher glanced over his shoulder. They were alone in the dark tunnel, but he could hear the echo of footsteps in the darkness.

He came to a halt and waited for the others.

"We don't need to wait. I can get you back to the village." Fencer sounded confident. "I won't let anything happen to you."

He glanced at her as if she were crazy. The girl didn't have any armor or weapons at all. She was always following Watcher around, appearing where she wasn't wanted . . . or needed. He knew the young girl had a crush on him. Since he'd saved her life by giving her a golden apple to heal her from a terrible fall, Fencer had been infatuated with Watcher, to the annoyance of a lot of people, especially his girlfriend, Planter. Watcher knew he should push Fencer away more assertively, but she was just a kid. And besides, having a cheering section wasn't the worst thing for his ego. With his history of being the smallest and scrawniest in the village, having someone tell him he was great was a nice change.

Planter and Blaster emerged from the shadows and ran into the circle of light generated by the magic pulsing through Watcher's body.

"Nice of you to wait for us." Blaster smiled.

"Well, I wanted to—"

"We didn't want to go too fast for you two," Fencer explained. "Watcher thought it best to wait so he could protect you."

"Oh, did he now?" Planter gave him an annoyed look.

"No, I didn't think that," Watcher stammered. "It was just . . . well . . ."

"This whole situation," Blaster said, pointing at Planter and Fencer with one of his knives, "seems to be working out great for you." He gave Watcher another smile, then laughed, amused by Watcher's predicament.

"I'm gonna remember this if our roles are ever reversed," Watcher said to Blaster with a snarl.

"Never gonna happen, my friend." Blaster seemed even more amused.

"What situation? What's he talking about?" Fencer was clueless.

Blaster laughed again, then took off running. "Planter, you coming?"

"No, I'll stay with my *boyfriend*." She glared at Fencer. "You should go with Blaster."

"I'm okay here, with Watcher."

Planter rolled her eyes.

"I heard that," Blaster chuckled from the darkness.

Grabbing Watcher by the sleeve, Planter pulled him forward. "Come on, let's get back to the village and talk with Mapper."

They ran through the passage in an uneasy silence, Planter glaring at the oblivious Fencer now and then. Eventually, they reached a section that was well-lit by torches; it was part of the ancient structure the villagers used on a regular basis.

"Fencer, it would be really helpful if you found Mapper and told him to meet us in the main tower." Watcher smiled at the girl.

"Okay, I'll do it right away!" The young girl took off running.

The silence became oppressive as Watcher waited for Planter to blast him with complaints, but she stayed quiet. They walked slowly through the passage, the silence getting louder and louder, until he couldn't take it anymore.

"It's not my fault she's always following me around."

"And why do you think that is?"

"I don't know." Watcher looked back at Planter, trying to sound innocent.

"Do you remember saving her life by giving her that golden apple after she fell?"

"Yeah."

"And then she gave you a big hug when she was better." Planter leaned a little closer, her voice soft and calm. "The hug was uncomfortably long; do you remember that?"

Watcher nodded.

"And now she follows you around wherever you go. Why do you think Fencer's doing that?" Her voice was getting louder.

"How should I know? I'm not a mind reader."

"But you're also not an idiot." Planter sounded aggravated. "Maybe you should use your 'wizarding powers' and cast a spell or something so you can figure it out."

She stormed off, leaving Watcher baffled.

"What did I do?" He glanced around, hoping for some support from someone, but he was all alone in the passage.

Watcher knew why Fencer was treating him this way, but he just didn't have the heart to hurt the young girl; he didn't want to be a monster.

If only I could—, he thought, but the voice of the Flail burst into his mind.

Tell them! The voice from the magical weapon echoed in his head. *Tell them about the Broken Eight . . . now!*

He sighed, then headed for the main tower.

CHAPTER 4

Watcher ran through the ancient structure, the many redstone lanterns embedded in the walls and ceiling casting a warm orange glow. As he moved closer to the main tower, he saw more NPCs moving about, doing chores, and just living their lives in this subterranean structure.

The Wizard's Tower had been built centuries ago, before the Great War, and the wizards had hidden many artifacts in it, likely to keep them out of the hands of the monsters. Watcher had found his enchanted sword, Needle, in the Tower, as well as countless other enchanted artifacts, the Amulet of Planes being the most recent.

I wonder why Planter could detect its presence and I couldn't? Watcher wondered, perplexed.

"Here he comes," someone shouted up ahead.

A group of villagers stood impatiently around the entrance to the main tower; apparently, Fencer had done more than just bring Mapper.

He slowed when he reached the congregation. Suddenly, Fencer emerged from the crowd.

"Let him through . . . let him through." She moved in front of Watcher and pushed the other NPCs out of the way. "Move out of the way. Watcher has important stuff to talk about with Mapper."

The other villagers murmured and spoke quietly; the feeling of anxiety and tension was thick in the air.

Watcher followed Fencer through the crowd until he made it into the tower. Villagers were packed together here as well. He glanced up at the structure and, as always, felt humbled by its construction. The tower rose about fifty blocks into the air, its walls decorated with different colors of stained glass. Near the top, the sunlight streamed through the windows, splashing an artist's palette of colors and hues onto the walls of the tower, though the lower windows were still dark. All of the windows would have seen the sunlight when the structure was first built, but, sometime during the Great War between the wizards and warlocks, the entire Wizard's Tower had fallen into some kind of gigantic hole. Now, just the very top part of the tower was above ground, leaving the rest buried beneath a now-thriving forest.

"Watcher, what's going on?" Mapper stood next to Watcher's father, Cleric. Both men had confused expressions on their wrinkled faces. "Fencer said there was an emergency and you were attacked by something. What was it? Spiders? Skeletons?"

"What?" He glanced at Fencer and scowled, but her face just lit up when she saw him looking at her.

"There was no attack." He turned away from her and faced his father. "At least not here."

The other villagers murmured, the tension growing.

"Then what happened, son?" Cleric moved closer to Watcher, stepping into a bright shaft of orange light streaming through one of the stained-glass windows. It made his gray hair appear gold.

"It's the king of the withers again, Krael. He's up to something, and it's not good."

"I think I can speak for everyone when I say we'd thought we'd seen the last of that monster." The voice came from the back of the tower; it was his sister, Winger. She pushed through the crowd and stood next to her dad. "When we defeated the spider warlord, you used the Fossil Bow of Destruction and fired an arrow at Krael. I guess I'd hoped it would have destroyed him."

"Well, apparently it didn't." Another voice boomed from behind.

Watcher turned and found Cutter moving toward him, with the other villagers quickly moving aside to make room for the big NPC warrior. At his side shuffled Er-Lan, the zombie who had been adopted by the village, and who was likely Watcher's best friend.

"What's all this about an emergency?" Cutter's steel-gray eyes bored into Watcher. They were, as always, filled with courage and confidence.

"Ok . . . well . . . we were in some of the passages and—"

"Watcher was attacked by some kind of invisible monster." Fencer stepped forward and smiled at Watcher proudly, as if she'd just saved him from something.

The other villagers all started talking at once, many of them glancing about and pulling out their weapons, worried about possible invisible attackers.

"Hold on . . . hold on." Watcher held his hands up in the air, his glowing arms instantly silencing the other villagers. "That's *not* what happened."

The NPCs grew quiet. When they were calm, he continued. "I felt something terrible happen with my magic; it must have come through the fabric of Minecraft somehow. Anyway, I used a magical artifact to investigate and was able to see the king of the withers. He was moving down a snowy mountain with what looked like a huge castle or prison or something in the background. With him were a bunch of zombies all clad in gold armor and with a bunch of huge wolves with them. They were—"

"How many were seen?" Er-Lan's voice shook a little.

"Ahh . . . what?"

"How many zombies were in the vision?" Er-Lan moved closer, eyes wide.

"There were eight of them, and they all wore the same golden armor, which sparkled, as if it were enchanted. But the really weird thing was their helmets. They were each—"

"Each helmet was made to resemble a different creature." Er-Lan said it as a statement, not a question.

"Yes! How did you know that?"

Er-Lan sighed. "They are the Broken—the Broken Eight." The zombie's voice cracked with fear. "This is bad . . . this is very bad."

"Er-Lan, what are the Broken Eight?" Cleric asked, putting an arm around the zombie, trying to calm him.

"They were created by the monster warlocks at the end of the Great War. Zombie parents tell the story to children, to make them do chores or behave." Er-Lan's voice grew quieter, making the villagers move closer to hear. "They were living weapons, created to hunt down the NPC wizards and destroy them. But the magic used to create the Eight was too strong. Their creators could not control the ancient zombie warriors, and soon, they turned on the warlocks as well. The stories say they were jailed in the Eternal Prison, to be kept there until they perished, but it seems they have returned."

"Yep." Watcher nodded. "They destroyed a village near the prison." Watcher glanced up at his father. "There were no survivors. I saw the whole thing using the Eye of Searching. But somehow, Krael knew I was watching. I don't know what he's up to, but it's not good."

"Er-Lan knows." The zombie stepped directly in front of Watcher. "Krael still seeks the Cave of Slumber."

"What does the Broken Eight have to do with the Cave of Slumber?" Mapper asked.

"Perhaps the wither king thinks the broken magic woven into these zombies will break the enchantments in the Cave of Slumber." Er-Lan turned, looking at all the faces staring at him. "Krael will try to free the wither army with these zombies, and Er-Lan believes it may be possible. There is great and terrible magic woven into the Broken Eight."

"If Krael is successful, then things are gonna get really bad, really fast," Blaster said, sounding worried.

"The wither king will try to get the Broken Eight to the Hall of Planes." Er-Lan glanced at Mapper. "The Hall is mentioned in many books."

Mapper nodded. "Yes, I've read about the Hall of Planes. There, it's possible to travel to different planes of existence throughout the Pyramid of Servers. Er-Lan, is that how Krael will try to reach the Cave of Slumber?"

The zombie nodded.

"Wait . . . did you say 'Planes?'" Planter reached into her inventory and pulled out the amulet she'd just found. "This thing is called the Amulet of Planes; it told me so."

"It told you so?" Winger asked. "That sounds a little crazy . . . like something Watcher would say." She smiled at her brother.

Watcher just scowled.

"I know it's strange, but that's what I heard." Planter turned to Mapper. "Have you ever read about something called the Amulet of Planes?"

The old man reached up and ran his fingers across his bald head, as if he were straightening hair the years had long-since removed. Only a thin circle of gray hair surrounded the old man's head; his scalp shiny as a quartz block.

"I do remember something about it." Mapper leaned forward and stared at the sparkling artifact. "But I thought it would be a key, not a necklace."

"It's an amulet," Planter corrected.

"Yes . . . yes, of course, an amulet."

"Why did you think it was a key?" Watcher asked.

"Well . . . let me remember." Mapper stroked his nonexistent hair again. "As I recall, it's supposed to unlock a door of some kind."

"It must unlock the door to the Hall of Planes," Watcher said. "And if it can unlock it, then it can lock it too." He glanced at Cutter. "I'm sure Krael plans to get to the Cave of Slumber and release his wither army. If we can get to that door before him, then we can make sure it's locked, and the king of the withers will never reach the Cave of Slumber."

"There's a lot of 'ifs' in there." Cutter gazed down at Watcher, his height dwarfing everyone in the room. "You sure about this?"

Watcher glanced around. Everyone was staring at him, expecting some kind of heroic statement, but all he could think to say was one thing:

"Yep."

"Watcher, you're so brave." Fencer tried to get to his side, but Planter stepped in front of her and rolled her eyes.

"Inspiring speech, Watcher," Blaster said sarcastically, giving his friend a smile.

"Then let's do this," Cutter said. "I say we take about a dozen soldiers with us. A large force would be slow and hard to move quietly through the land. We don't want to attract any unnecessary attention."

"Agreed." Watcher turned to his father and sister. "I'd feel better if you two stayed here and made sure all the villagers are safe."

"Awwww . . . I want to go, too." Winger looked upset.

"We can't do this if we're all worried about everyone else back here in the village. I need you here so you can set up defenses in case we trigger some kind of monster retribution. It happened with the skeletons and the spiders in the past; why wouldn't it happen this time as well?"

Winger sighed. "Fine, but only if you agree to a couple of things."

"What?"

"First, I want you to take my best Elytra." She pulled a set of wings from her inventory. They sparkled with enchantments, making the fragile things glow like Watcher's arms. "They have a mending enchantment, so if you don't hurt them too badly, they'll be able to repair themselves. Use them when walking just won't do."

"Great." Watcher took the wings, then held out his hands as if expecting to get more. "What else?"

In response, Winger pushed her brother aside and stood before Planter. "Planter, I want you to take my bow. It has the *Flame* and *Infinity* enchantments on it. You'll never run out of arrows, and having fire arrows always seems to be handy."

"Thanks, I'll take good care of it." Planter took the bow from the girl's hands.

Winger glanced down at the bow and gave it a wistful look, as if she didn't expect ever to see it again. "No, it'll take good care of you." She gave Planter a forced smile, then stepped back.

"Okay," Cutter boomed. "Let's get ready to go."

"Yeah . . . let's gather our equipment and get ready," Watcher said, trying to sound as confident as Cutter, but it was difficult, especially with the images in his mind of the Broken Eight storming through that village. They had been like an unstoppable force of nature. Would their band of warriors be strong enough to weather that storm? They were likely to find out.

CHAPTER 5

Krael floated through the air, his dark, protruding spine just barely skimming the ground. The Broken Eight ran next to him, easily keeping pace with the wither king, their direwolves loping along beside them with hungry eyes and snapping jaws. Behind each zombie, a trail of charred footsteps marked the ground where the broken spells wrapped around the ancient warriors had damaged the very fabric of Minecraft.

With the village destroyed behind them, the wither king knew he now had a chance to get to know his new allies better. He looked at the one with the dragon-shaped helmet.

"You're the one in command of the Broken Eight, correct?"

"This zombie commands, yes."

"And you said your name is Ya-Sik?"

The zombie nodded, and the wither king's left skull chuckled. "Zombies and their names . . . they're so strange."

Ya-Sik said nothing.

"What are the other names?" Right asked, her voice soft and soothing as she stared down at the monsters.

"Wi-Sik, Vu-Sik, Ur-Sik, Tu-Sik, Ra-Sik, Pe-Sik and

Ni-Sik." Each one of the zombie warriors stood tall and proud when Ya-Sik spoke their names.

"All of your names end with Sik," Krael said. "What's that about?"

"A zombie's last name is the family name. The first name shows the rank." Ya-Sik lifted his chin in pride. "The closer to the end of the alphabet, the higher the rank. Any can challenge for leadership and take Ya-Sik's name, but all know better."

"Have any of the Eight tried to challenge you in the past?" Right asked.

Ya-Sik laughed. "One tried a long time ago, but Ni-Sik was not strong enough. The scar across the face of that zombie is a reminder."

He glared at one of the zombies with a helmet resembling that of a wolf's head, and the zombie removed it and stared back at his commander. A long scar ran down the left side of his face, clearly a memento from the challenge that had ended poorly for him.

"Put your helmet back on, Ni-Sik." The zombie commander ordered, scowling.

Ni-Sik acquiesced and replaced his helmet, and Ya-Sik turned back to face Krael.

"Where is it the king of the withers is leading the Broken Eight?" There was an almost challenging tone to Ya-Sik's voice. "It was understood that revenge against the wizards is of paramount importance."

"The zombies are not very respectful." Left glared at the zombie. "Don't they know who we are?"

"Left, be quiet for a change." Right glared at the skull.

"*Both* of you be quiet!" Center's voice boomed across the landscape, silencing the skulls. The wither king gave each an angry glare, the Crown of Skulls glowing bright upon his head, then turned his attention to the zombie leader. "We are heading to the Cave of Slumber. There, we will release an army of withers trapped by the wizards at the end of the Great War. Once they are free, we will rain flaming skulls down upon the NPCs."

"But revenge against the wizards was promised." Ya-Sik stopped running and held his gold sword in the air. The other zombies stopped with him. "Did the wither lie to the Broken Eight?"

"Don't be a fool, zombie." Krael floated higher into the air, out of reach of their puny swords. One of the wolves growled at him, but the king of the withers paid it no heed. "The last remaining wizard will undoubtedly follow us to the Cave. He already knows of our plans, and is probably heading there now. We will have ample opportunity to destroy the boy-wizard and his friends."

"How does the wither know this?" Ya-Sik asked doubtfully.

"It's true." Right's voice was, as usual, calm and soothing. It gave her words a sense of importance. "The wizard saw us after we released the Broken Eight. He was using some kind of enchanted artifact. In fact, he's probably watching us right now."

"The longer we stand here and talk, the stronger the boy-wizard becomes," Center said. Krael's three skulls all stared down at the zombie leader. "You'll never find this wizard without me." The wither started floating backward, continuing to the east. "Now, are you coming with me, or will I get to destroy the boy-wizard on my own?"

"We will follow, but tell the Eight where this Cave of Slumber can be found." Ya-Sik lowered his sword and nodded to the other zombies. The monsters began running again, keeping up with the wither, seemingly unfazed by the effort.

"Our destination, right now, is the Hall of Planes." Krael waited to see if the zombies knew the name; the blank stares on their faces suggested they didn't. He curved around a tall oak tree, the green leaves brushing his shoulder, then continued.

"The Hall of Planes is a construction made by both the wizards and warlocks before the war began. It is a place where one can travel from one plane of existence to another, moving throughout the Pyramid of Servers that makes up the Minecraft universe."

"Pyramid of Servers?" Ya-Sik was confused.

"I don't know exactly what it means. All I know is, that's what it's called." The wither ducked under some low branches, moving closer to the ground. Left turned to watch the zombies and direwolves while they were near the ground. "In some ancient books written by the wizards, I found references to the Hall of Planes. Apparently, the wizards put the Cave of Slumber on a different plane of existence from this one so that it would be difficult to find."

"But those ancient fools had no idea who would be looking for it," Left said. "Being on a different plane won't stop us."

Center smiled deviously. "We'll go to that plane to find our army, then bring destruction to the Far Lands."

Ya-Sik nodded. He glanced at the other zombies as they ran; they too nodded.

"Very well," the zombie said. "Where is the entrance to this Hall of Planes?"

Krael ducked under another branch, then rose from the ground, out of reach again from any weapons. "The ancient texts spoke of an entrance to the Hall of Planes hidden under a village well. That's why we destroyed that village near your prison, so I could blast the well and look beneath it."

"And we also got to destroy some villagers, too." Left grinned.

The other skulls chuckled. The Broken Eight remained silent.

"Where is the wither heading now?" Ya-Sik asked again.

"There is another village to the east," Center explained. "It's near an ancient structure buried in the desert. That seems like a likely place for the entrance to the Hall of Planes."

"And when the wither finds this new village, will the

NPCs be destroyed?" Ya-Sik glared up at the wither king as if challenging him.

"Of course." All three skulls smiled maliciously. "The villagers are our enemy, just as the wizard is. We will destroy them, just because they are there." Krael thought about his wife, Kora, imprisoned in the Cave for all those years, and his rage grew. "The wizards will pay for what they have done. They thought they won the Great War, but all they did was put it on pause for a century or two. We will bring the war back and teach the NPCs what it means to suffer."

The zombies cheered and banged their shining swords against their curved shields, running even faster as the king of the withers accelerated his pace, anxious to find the next village and punish it.

CHAPTER 6

Watcher glanced at the darkening forest as he guided his horse past tall oaks and bright birches. The western sky grew angry as splashes of red and orange stretched across the horizon, shining warm hues upon the Far Lands. The rays of light turned the bright green forest to something moody and mysterious. Long shadows stretched from the base of the trees, reaching toward the eastern horizon as if trying to grasp at the yet-to-arrive moon. To the east, the sky was a jeweled tapestry as the stars emerged for their evening performance. With the colorful view overhead and the thick aroma of leaves and wood around them, the world seemed brimming with vitality and life.

"Let's slow down and let the horses rest." Cutter raised a thick, muscular arm, then slowed his mount, the rest of the company doing the same. He glanced at Watcher. "Now, tell me again why you think we'll find the wither king heading this way?"

"Well . . . it's not me, it's Planter." Watcher pointed at his girlfriend. "Tell him and don't be shy." The boy-wizard smiled at her. "I listened to you before, just like I'll always listen and believe; that's what a boyfriend does."

Cutter rolled his eyes. "What . . . spill it. We all need to know what's going on."

"Well . . . it's about that amulet I found in the Wizard's Tower." Planter glanced around as more NPCs brought their horses closer to hear.

"What about it?" Blaster asked. "It looked like just some kind of necklace, that's all."

"No, it's enchanted," Watcher said, jumping to her defense. "We all saw it glowing, you know, like my arms. It must be magical . . . like me."

Blaster glanced at Cutter and chuckled, the big warrior doing the same.

"Watcher, you don't need to defend me. I can take care of myself." Planter reached out and grasped his hand in hers and squeezed it, then let go and faced the others. "The Amulet of Planes is whispering to me."

"Whispering to you?" Mapper moved his horse forward, so he was next to her. "That's fantastic."

"I know." She smiled and blushed. "Anyway, it's telling me the location of the Hall of Planes. It says to follow the rising sun until we reach the desert, then look beneath the well that lies between the dual dunes." An embarrassed expression came over her face. "I'm not sure what all that means, other than the rising sun part: we need to keep going to the east until we find a desert."

"That makes perfect sense. Can you show me the Amulet again?" Mapper was excited, like a child receiving gifts on Awakening day.

Planter pulled it out from beneath her enchanted chainmail armor and held it out. The reflective square of metal at the end of the silvery chain was bathed in iridescent light, with sparkles dancing about its edges, as if it had been made of the stars twinkling overhead. The blood-red gemstone at the center seemed lit with fire from within, making it glow unnaturally bright for a ruby.

"This artifact must have been made by one of the great wizards." Er-Lan adjusted himself in the saddle, uncomfortable on the horse's back. He patted the creature on the neck, then dismounted and let the animal rest. Others followed the monster's lead.

The leaves of a nearby fern swayed back and forth, drawing everyone's attention away from Planter and to the ground as a group of rabbits, likely a mother and a couple of babies, moved through the forest. Er-Lan bent down and picked up one of the bunnies, stroking its soft fur with his green hand.

"How did you do that?" a villager named Builder asked, amazed. "Rabbits are impossible to catch."

The NPC reached out to grab one of the bunnies, but instantly it bolted, scurrying away so fast it was hard to see where it had gone.

The zombie shrugged. "Er-Lan has a way with animals."

"I guess you do." Mapper nodded.

Setting the rabbit on the ground, Er-Lan nudged it along, causing it to hop toward its companions. It rejoined the others, then the family of bunnies hopped away into the now-dark forest, the silvery rays of the moon that filtered through the trees offering little in the way of illumination.

"There are all kinds of interesting things hidden away within you, Er-Lan," Planter said, smiling at the monster.

The zombie just shrugged again.

"He really does have a way with animals." Watcher was proud of his friend. He glanced at the NPC who tried to catch the rabbit. "You're Builder, right?"

The villager nodded, his long brown hair swaying across his face.

"I saw you hugging some kids before we left the Wizard's Tower; were they your children?" Watcher asked.

"No, they're my brother's kids. But I love them as if they were my own." Builder smiled. "I'd do anything for those kids; that's why I'm here."

"I don't understand," Planter said.

"My brother—his name's Builder as well; we're twins—anyway, he's hurt from a fall off the roof of a house and couldn't go with us." Builder stood up a little taller when he started talking about his brother. "He'd be here with us if he could; so I went in his place. I figure if I can help destroy this wither king, then Builder's boy and girl will be safer. It's the least I could do. My niece and nephew are the light of my life. If anything plans on hurting them, they'll have to go through me first."

"And us, too," Watcher said.

"So let's go find us this wither king that's threatening us and crush it." Builder's voice resonated with confidence and strength.

"I like the way he thinks," Cutter said, patting the villager on the back.

Suddenly, sticks cracked in the darkening forest, and they all heard the sound of heavy feet moving through the leaves and twigs.

"What kind of animal is that?" Planter asked the zombie, sounding worried.

"Not a rabbit." Er-Lan's voice was barely a whisper. Slowly, the zombie's claws extended from each finger as the monster prepared for battle.

"Maybe the spiders know we're here?" Cutter drew his sword as he handed his reins to Mapper.

Watcher drew Needle and moved toward Planter's horse, but she was already moving toward the noise, her enchanted bow held ready for battle.

The rest of the warriors quietly drew their weapons and spread out, each watching the others' backs. More sticks cracked. The NPCs all turned toward the sound, the warriors standing in groups of two or three. They moved quietly through the woods, the only light coming from their enchanted weapons and armor and Watcher's arms.

A horse whinnied nervously as the thump of something dismounting floated through the air. Leaves and sticks crunched as the *thing* approached. All the villagers froze in place and hid behind trees, their enchanted weapons, armor, and glowing arms held close to the thick trunks of the oak trees to hide their light.

The mysterious thing moved closer, its crackling steps now only a handful of blocks from them.

"Hold your fire until I give the word," Watcher whispered. "Pass the word."

The warriors relayed the message to their neighbors. Archers slackened their bows, but still held them ready to draw and fire.

Watcher glanced at Cutter, nodded, then leaped out from behind his tree, yelling his battle cry as Cutter and the others did the same. A high-pitched scream pierced through the dark forest as he charged forward, the glow of his arms and weapon casting a lavender glow upon the scene. Planter and Blaster closed in from the other side, the glow from Planter's bow adding more illumination to the scene.

Standing in the center of the iridescent circle of light was a young girl with long blond hair, tied in a ponytail down her back: Fencer.

"What are you doing here?!" Cutter was furious.

"Well . . . umm . . . it's just—"

"We might have thought you were a monster and attacked you," Planter scolded.

"Maybe she is a monster . . . in disguise." Blaster glanced at Watcher and laughed. "Let's get back to the horses."

The warriors put away their weapons, many of them shaking their heads in disbelief, then turned and walked back to their horses.

"Fencer, what were you thinking?" Watcher was furious.

"Well . . . I was afraid for you after you left. You need someone to look after you while you're chasing these monsters." Fencer took a step toward Watcher. "Who's gonna do that for you if I'm not here?"

Planter coughed an obvious cough, then glared at the young girl. "You shouldn't be here. What we're doing is dangerous. It's warrior's work, and you don't know the first thing about fighting." She glanced at her boyfriend. "Watcher, you need to take care of this . . . now!"

And then she turned and stormed off, heading back to the horses.

Watcher just stood there, staring at Fencer, speechless.

"Are you mad at me?" Fencer stepped closer and put a hand on Watcher's arm. "I came here because no one understands you like I do. You're a great wizard, and they don't respect you as they should . . . as I do. I can help, really I can."

The faint sound of a zombie's sorrowful moan floated through the forest. Fencer jumped and moved closer to Watcher, now holding onto his arm with two hands.

"Well, I can't send you back now with monsters running around." Watcher sighed.

"I knew you'd want me here." She smiled, then spun around and ran to her horse. Pulling on the reins, she brought the animal back to Watcher. "You don't need to worry. I brought enough food for both of us. I'll take care of you the way you *should* be taken care of." She lowered her voice to a whisper. "I know how important you *really* are."

And with that, she ran to the others with her horse in tow, leaving Watcher standing there, frustrated.

What am I supposed to do? Watcher thought. *I can't send Fencer home at night with monsters around. She'll have to stay with us. But I don't think Planter's gonna be very happy about it.*

"Maybe I can keep the peace between everyone while we're chasing Krael," Watcher whispered to himself, but he didn't feel very hopeful. He knew this problem was only going to get worse.

Glancing down at his arms, Watcher pondered if his magic ability could help somehow.

Magic should only be used on other NPCs with great care. The mystical voice came from the Flail of Regrets, but it did not frighten him. Watcher had come to terms with the fact that some kind of living entity resided inside the weapon . . . and he could talk to it.

Then how do I solve this problem? Watcher asked the enchanted relic.

By being a true wizard.

Sometimes—like now—the thoughts from the Flail made no sense.

Watcher sighed. He could hear the rest of the party getting mounted, the horses' hooves stomping the ground impatiently. Turning, he headed back to his companions, his thoughts focused again on the battles to come.

CHAPTER 7

Krael smiled at the eastern horizon as a blood-red stain spread across the sky in anticipation of the sun emerging from its long evening nap. Sadly, the crimson only remained for an instant before fading to a bright orange. The warm dawn light coated the sands of the desert with colorful hues, but neither the king of the withers nor the Broken Eight appreciated the spectacular show.

They'd left the forest just before sunrise and were now moving with great haste across the parched sands. Even here, the angry magic embedded in the monsters' golden boots still damaged the ground, leaving a trail of charred footsteps in the sand to show where the zombies had stepped. Behind the group, the tall, snowy peak that held the Eternal Prison was still visible, though it was mixed in with the haze of Minecraft, making the frozen peak and the jail difficult to see.

"Ya-Sik is glad to see that frozen mountain fading from view." The zombie commander glared over his shoulder at the peak as if it were a fierce enemy. The direwolf loping next to him growled in agreement. "The Broken Eight spent too many centuries in those prison cells."

"All the more reason to seek out revenge upon the wizards," the right skull on Krael's broad shoulders said.

"It was not just wizards who trapped the Eight in those cells." The zombie's rage was barely contained. "Others helped."

Many of the zombie warriors nodded their scarred heads, each glaring back at the distant jail. Krael could feel the anger frothing up from within the monsters and wolves, their thirst for vengeance growing every second.

"I understand your suffering, my friends," Center said.

"How could the wither understand?" Vu-Sik asked. The zombie faced the wither, its blaze-shaped helmet pointing toward him.

The king of the withers grew silent for a moment. He veered around a cactus, the sharp spines sparkling in the morning light, but the zombies ignored it; they just walked over the prickly plant, their enchanted golden armor protecting them from its sharp thorns.

"They took my wife," Krael hissed in a low voice.

"What?" Ya-Sik moved up next to the wither.

"I said they took my wife." Center looked down at the zombie, its dark eyes filled with hate. "The NPC wizards constructed the Cave of Slumber and lured the withers into it, my wife, Kora, included. When I uncovered their plot, I was able to flee, but none of the other withers escaped. The wizards used some kind of magical arti-fact to lure the withers into the cave, and before they knew it, they were asleep and trapped . . . forever." Another cactus loomed near. Instead of veering around this one, Krael launched a flaming skull at it, blasting the green plant to dust and leaving a crater as the cac-tus's tombstone. The king of the withers hoped the act would lessen his rage and pain, but it had no effect. "I barely escaped the trap and swore to release my kin and my wife from their unjust imprisonment." The three skulls glared down at the zombies. "We will lay waste to the Far Lands when my brothers and sisters . . . and Kora . . . are free."

"It seems Krael has good reason to hate this boy-wizard," the zombie commander said, nodding in understanding.

"He has interrupted my plans too many times and will not get another chance. When we find the—"

Just then, the sounds of activity floated across the desert, silencing the wither king.

Krael lowered himself to the ground and approached a large sand dune that loomed up ahead.

"The sounds are coming from the other side of the dune," Right whispered, her melodic voice soothing some of Center's rage.

"It's the villager I was looking for." Center gave the other skulls a satisfied smile.

"What is it the king of the withers is searching for?" one of the zombie warriors asked, this one wearing a helmet shaped like a creeper's head.

"The wizards hid the Cave of Slumber on a different plane of existence. These planes are all part of the Pyramid of Servers that holds together all of Minecraft. The Cave of Slumber lies in one of these planes."

"How does one travel from this plane to another?" Ya-Sik asked.

"The wizards built something called the Hall of Planes." Center's voice was barely a whisper. "In that hall, we will find countless portals, each going to a different plane of existence. It is there that we will find the right portal."

"But surely this Hall is guarded?" Ra-Sik asked, his enderman-shaped helmet staring at the wither.

"And the portals are likely locked, to restrict access," another zombie said.

Krael nodded. "Both are true, but what the wizards don't know is that the overpowered magic spells used to create the Broken Eight will allow us to enter the Hall of Planes. All we need do is find the entrance to the Hall and force our way in; the door will yield to the Broken Eight. Once we're in the Hall, I'll be able to feel which portal leads to the Cave of Slumber." Center smiled an evil toothy smile. "You will be the keys that will open these doorways and allow us to destroy all the fools in the Far Lands."

Ya-Sik smiled.

"Then why has the wither stopped here, in this desert?" Wi-Sik asked, his helmet, shaped like the head of a ghast, staring defiantly at Krael.

The wither king wanted to knock those stupid helmets off the zombies; they gave him the creeps. But he knew they were part of the key that would unlock the magical doorways in the Hall of Planes.

"Ancient writings said the door to the Hall of Planes was hidden under a well near the Eternal Prison. The first village we destroyed had no doorway, but there is a village on the other side of these dunes." Krael cast his gaze upon Ya-Sik. "I thought, perhaps the Broken Eight would be so kind as to annihilate this village, and then I'll destroy the well and see what's hidden underneath."

Ya-Sik's smile grew even bigger. He nodded, then glanced at his zombies; their eyes all lit up with excitement, their direwolves pacing back and forth, anxious for battle as well.

"Go, my friends . . . feast on their XP." Krael's voice boomed across the dry landscape.

The ancient zombie warriors sprinted over the sand dune, a charred trail of footprints following each. Their direwolves ran next to them, the huge animals howling with angry glee.

They fell upon the unsuspecting village like a storm of razor-sharp swords and pointed teeth; the NPCs were helpless against them. And all the while, Krael just floated up into the air to watch . . . and laugh.

CHAPTER 8

Watcher ached with a deep weariness, not just of body, but of spirit as well. Fencer and Planter had been glaring at each other all through the night, and his girlfriend's glances toward him clearly suggested he had to do something . . . but what?

I can't send Fencer back to their village without sending a couple of soldiers with her, he thought. *But keeping her here doesn't seem like a good idea, either.*

Watcher had no idea what to do.

He looked around wearily and took in his surroundings. They'd ridden hard all night, and everyone was exhausted. The villagers had made it through the forest until they came across their enemy's tracks. Now, they'd followed them through the quiet woods and into afternoon, the sun already past its zenith.

"Watcher . . . look out!"

He stopped daydreaming and looked ahead; his horse was heading straight for an oak tree. He pulled on the reins at the last second, causing the animal to veer to the left, narrowly avoiding the thick trunk.

"Maybe you should pay attention," Cutter chided.

Watcher could feel his cheeks turning red.

"Well, it's not like we need Watcher's expert tracking

skills to follow our friends' trail." Blaster pointed at the sandy ground, where footprints were burned into the surface of Minecraft, damaging the landscape.

"That does make it easier," Cutter admitted. "What do you think is making those tracks?"

"The Eight." Er-Lan's quiet voice was almost like a moan, drawn out and sad. "It is the mark of the Broken Eight. All zombies have heard the stories about the terrible enchantments needed to create these warriors. The evil magic used to bring them into existence cannot be contained, even within their golden armor. It leaks out and scars the land."

"Great . . . you're making me really excited to meet these creatures."

"The forest is ending up ahead." Planter pointed with her shimmering axe, then glanced at Watcher. She neither smiled nor frowned.

What's that supposed to mean? Watcher was even more confused.

As they passed from the forest to the desert biome, heat slammed into them with the force of a giant's hammer. Instantly, sweat poured down Watcher's face, the tiny cubes of salty moisture managing to get past his thick unibrow and seep into his eyes, stinging. He wanted to take off his armor, but knew it wasn't a good idea; the Broken Eight or wither king could be nearby.

They continued trudging across the rolling sand dunes, following the black footprints across the desert sand, all of them anxious to catch up to their prey, but Watcher could feel the nervousness of his comrades building. These were the most dangerous monsters in all of Minecraft; Watcher was afraid of what would happen when they finally caught them.

"Look, it seems as if they stopped here, behind this sand dune." Mapper leaned so far out of the saddle to stare at the footprints that he almost fell off his horse. Many of the soldiers laughed.

"Maybe you should try to stay *on* your horse," Blaster suggested with a good-natured grin.

The old man blushed and nodded, embarrassed.

Watcher glanced up at the sun high overhead; its heat pounded down mercilessly on the NPCs. His armor was hot to the touch, and the air burned his throat as he breathed. It was a harsh environment, but they had to follow the trail, no matter where it led.

On the ground ahead were the remains of a cactus, its green, spiny body shattered and burned by the charred footprints.

One of the Broken Eight must have crushed it, Watcher thought. *But why would it want to do that? Maybe they—*

"There's a village on the other side of this dune," a forward scout shouted from atop a sandy mound. The NPC sat on a light brown horse, his leather armor a dirty white, courtesy of Blaster; wearing it, the villager and his mount blended in with the pale surroundings of the desert, making them hard to see when they stood still. "Hurry . . . something's happened to them!"

"What do you think he means by that?" Watcher asked.

"I don't know," Planter said from behind him.

He turned and smiled at her.

"I'm sure you'll figure it out. You always do." Fencer rode up next to him and matched his pace, guiding her horse so close to his, their legs were brushing against each other. She gave him an adoring grin.

"Grrr . . ." Planter growled like a zombie, then snapped her reins and galloped up the hill, her face a visage of anger as she passed.

"Planter seems so angry all the time," Fencer said softly, just for Watcher's ears. "She should be more respectful . . . in fact, they all should be more respectful to you. You're a wizard, after all." She leaned toward him, bringing her horse even closer. "I know how important you are. I'll never mistreat you . . . not like the others do."

"Look, Fencer, you need to understand something." Watcher paused. She had such an innocent expression on her face; he felt like he was about to do something mean and hurt her. He glanced ahead at Planter. Her blond hair shone bright against the afternoon sun; it was beautiful. He turned back to Fencer. "You see, I'm with—"

"Oh no! Watcher, come quick!" Planter didn't even turn to look at him, she just shouted and then rode down the other side of the dune.

A jolt of fear surged through Watcher's veins, and he instantly nudged his horse into a gallop, then into a sprint as he charged up the sandy mound. When he reached the top, his heart sank.

Strewn across the sands were the remains of the village. Charred footsteps could be seen all throughout the area, as well as paw prints embedded in the sand from the vicious direwolves.

Riding down the dune as fast as he could, he caught up with Planter, then shot past her.

"We need to search for survivors," Watcher shouted.

Someone else yelled commands to the other NPCs, but Watcher wasn't listening; he was scanning the flat, sandy plain, looking for anyone moving or crying out for help. But the village seemed completely still . . . like a graveyard.

Leaping off his horse, Watcher dashed through the smoky ruins of what looked like a blacksmith's house. Only a couple of furnaces had survived the destruction; the rest of the house lay shattered, burnt to the ground. Running up to what resembled a baker's house, he kicked through the brittle remains, hoping to uncover someone hiding in the rubble, but there was no one. With panic rising in his soul, Watcher ran from house to house, digging through the wreckage, looking for any living thing.

It was hopeless.

The entire village had been erased from the surface of Minecraft, just like the one he'd seen when he used the Eye of Searching.

"Why would they do this?" Planter asked, choking back her emotions. "I don't understand."

"It is the Eight." Er-Lan moved toward Watcher, careful to step over the charred footprints left behind by the ancient warriors. "Their hatred for everything drove the Broken Eight to do this horrible thing. There is no plan here, no strategy or goal . . . just devastation. That is why these ancient warriors were put in the Eternal Jail. It was the only way to stop their destruction."

"But these people did nothing to them." A terrible sadness rose up from within Watcher, but mixed with it was also guilt. He should have been here to stop them. Even though he knew that to be impossible, he still felt responsible for this destruction.

These creatures may have been made by the monster warlocks hundreds of years ago, but this *wizard is gonna destroy them.* Watcher's thoughts raged with fury within his mind. He wanted to shout and scream, but it would not change what had happened.

There may be a way, the ancient voice from the Flail of Regrets whispered.

"What?" Watcher said.

"I didn't say anything," Blaster replied.

Watcher shook his head. *What did you say?* he asked the Flail with his thoughts.

There may be a way to stop the Broken Eight, the Flail said. *But it will take some thought. We'll likely need some friends from the old days.*

What are you talking about? Watcher asked, but the voice was gone.

"You okay?" Blaster put a hand on Watcher's shoulder, startling him and making him jump. "Sorry, didn't mean to scare you. Don't blast me with any of your magical powers." He smiled at Watcher.

"Sorry, I was talking to . . ." he lowered his voice and glanced around to be sure nobody was listening, "the Flail."

"Oh, of course, you were talking to that inanimate object in your inventory."

"It's really true; there's something alive inside it. I just don't fully understand, yet." Watcher pulled out the weapon and stared down at it. The enchanted weapon seemed almost as if it had just been made, even though it had been constructed hundreds of years ago, during the Great War; the leather-wrapped handle was worn, as if it had seen many battles, but the chain running from the handle to the spiked cube looked brand new, with each spike still razor sharp.

"Everyone, come over here." Cutter's booming voice carried across the desert with ease.

Watcher and Blaster ran toward what would have been the center of the village. Where the community's well had once stood was now just a huge, blackened crater. Watcher stood next to Cutter and stared down at the destruction.

"Why would they have destroyed the well like this?" Mapper started to move down into the crater, but Planter stopped the old man, pointing. "Did any of you notice what's at the bottom of the crater?"

Watcher held a hand over his eyes to shield them from the afternoon sun. They slowly adjusted to the dark, being able to pick out charred blocks of sandstone, sand, and gravel . . . and then he saw it: there were steps leading down into the darkness.

Soon everyone was pointing at them and talking all at once, but Watcher was instead looking at the landscape around them. On one side of the village was the large sand dune they had just crossed, but on the opposite side of the village was another one, identical in size and shape.

"The Dual Dunes." Watcher moved to Planter's side, then pointed. "Look . . . the Dual Dunes."

She followed his finger and stared at the two huge sandy mounds; then realization dawned on her face. "It's the entrance to the Hall of Planes."

Watcher nodded.

She pulled out the Amulet of Planes and found the red gemstone in the middle was blinking as if it had a heartbeat. Stepping into the crater, Planter moved closer to the dark stairway, Watcher at her side. The ancient relic pulsed faster and faster as they moved nearer to the shadowy passage.

Watcher glanced over his shoulder and nodded to the rest of the NPCs. "Everyone gather your things and leave your horses. Our path now leads downward."

The villagers moved down into the crater in complete silence. Watcher knew they were scared; he could somehow feel their tension through the enchantments pulsing through his body. When they reached the bottom of the crater, the company stood around the staircase, staring down at the steps disappearing into the darkness.

"This is the entrance to the Hall of Planes." Watcher turned and looked at each member of their party. "We have no idea what dangers we're heading toward, but as you saw from the village around us, these creatures must be stopped, and we're the only ones here. If we don't stop the zombie warriors *and* stop the king of the withers from releasing his army, then the Far Lands will likely be in the greatest danger it's faced since the Great War." He paused to let his words sink in. "We *can* do this if we work together. Now follow me."

"I'll be right behind you," Fencer shouted enthusiastically.

Watcher rolled his eyes as the rest of the warriors laughed.

Then, drawing his enchanted blade, Needle, he headed down into the darkness.

CHAPTER 9

Watcher moved down the dark stairway, his arms and his sword giving off their magical iridescent glow, making it bright enough to see the path before him. Other soldiers followed close behind, trying to stay within his circle of light, though Fencer was right behind him, talking incessantly.

"Good thing we've got the glowing boy up ahead," one of the soldiers behind them said softly, "or we wouldn't be able to see a thing in here." Some of the other warriors chuckled.

"They should be more respectful. I'm sure you're going to figure out how to stop these zombies," she prattled. "You're a wizard, after all, and they don't know who they're messing with. I know it's hard being a wizard, but I have faith in you."

"Can someone tell her to shut up?" Blaster's voice rang through the dark passage.

"Fencer, you need to be quiet." Watcher glanced over his shoulder and tried to frown, but when he saw the optimistic and confident expression on the girl's face, he smiled a little.

Fencer can be so annoying, he thought. *But I must say, it feels good having someone who understands me*

*and has confidence in my abilities. And besides, she's
right; I'm a wizard, and I should be treated with more
respect.*

Watcher continued to descend, going deeper and
deeper beneath the desert. Soon, the oppressive heat
was replaced with a cool, damp feeling, and the air
began smelling musty and old. He could tell this passage had been here for a long, long time, maybe even
since before the Great War.

His steps echoed off the cold stone walls, mixing
with the footsteps of the others. It sounded as if there
were hundreds of warriors with him.

If only that were true, Watcher thought wistfully.

After they'd descended for what seemed like hours,
a light started to emerge in the distance. It was a sparkling, luminous glow that outlined what appeared to be
the end of the stairs. As they neared, the sound of metal
grinding against metal, coupled with the pounding of
heavy footsteps, filled the passage.

"What's that noise?" Watcher whispered over his
shoulder.

"I don't know," Mapper replied. "Maybe some kind of
redstone or piston mechanism."

"But what about the footsteps?" Watcher glanced at
Planter; she had a scared expression on her face. "It
sounds like a giant down there."

She nodded, pulling out her enchanted axe and
shield. "Maybe more than one."

"I'm sure you'll take care of it, Watcher," Fencer said.
"You can do it . . . I know you can."

Watcher sighed as Planter rolled her eyes.

Holding a fist up into the air, Watcher stopped the
party, then slowly crept to the end of the staircase.
The pieces of an iron door lay on the last few steps, the
metal looking as if it had been peeled apart by something sharp and vicious.

The ground shook as the huge . . . whatever . . .
stomped about, the metallic grinding sound getting

louder. Watcher drew his sword, then glanced over his shoulder at the other warriors. They all pulled out their weapons, bows, and shields, getting ready to confront whatever was causing the sound.

With fear pulsing through his veins, Watcher moved to the end of the staircase and stepped out of the shadowy passage. Before him was a long hallway, the ground made of sparkling bedrock, the stone floor clearly enchanted with powerful spells. The subterranean corridor extended off into the distance, seemingly going forever.

On either side of the wide hallway stood large rings, big enough for a troop of soldiers to pass through. They were each made of enchanted iron blocks, with a sparkling green field filling each. Watcher instantly recognized these rings as portals, likely leading to the different planes of existence. They splashed a warm emerald glow on the ground but had no effect on the walls of the passage, which was strange. In fact, now that Watcher paid attention to them, the walls seemed completely black, as if they were made of . . . nothingness. It was tempting to reach out and touch the immaterial wall, but for some reason, that seemed dangerous.

"Who enters the Hall of Planes?" A voice suddenly boomed through the passage, making the very ground on which Watcher stood shake.

Just then, a massive creature made of iron blocks stepped away from one of the portals. Watcher hadn't noticed it before, as it blended in with the metallic ring, but, now that he saw it bathed in the sparkling light of the portal, Watcher instantly recognized the creature: an iron golem.

More of the huge giants stepped away from the portals and lumbered down the center of the Hall of Planes, heading straight for Watcher.

"We are the Guardians of the Hall," the creatures bellowed. "Only those with a key may enter. Leave now or abandon all hope."

Watcher put away his weapon, then held his hands over his head, showing he wasn't armed. "Look, I'm not carrying a weapon . . . I'm a friend."

At the sight of his glowing arms, the creatures stopped their advance, expressions of wondrous surprise on their metallic faces.

"A wizard," one of the golems said in awe. "He is not an enemy."

"If he is a wizard," growled another, "then he knows he must have the key or suffer the consequences." The discontented golem glanced at its comrades. "It is the law."

The other creatures nodded, then continued their slow advance, huge steel fists clenched at the ends of their muscular arms.

"Wait . . . wait!" someone shouted from the stairway.

Watcher glanced over his shoulder and saw Planter running out of the passage. She stopped at his side, then reached beneath her chain mail, searching frantically.

"Wait, we have the key!" Planter's voice sounded nervous.

The iron giants were getting closer, their fists making a crunching sound, as if there was something in their hands being pulverized to dust.

"It was right here a minute ago." Planter was starting to sound scared.

The golems were getting very close now, anger painted on each metal face.

One of the huge monsters kicked aside some iron blocks that lay on the ground in the vague shape of a golem. The cubes of metal slid across the bedrock, then hit the inky black wall and fell off the edge of the sparkling walkway, plummeting into the darkness.

Watcher noticed that a couple of the golems had scars across their arms and chest; deep gashes were sliced into their metal skins, the wounds jagged and rough. In some of the other golems' legs, deep teeth marks slashed across the metal, as if some kind of creature had taken bites out of them. Some of the guardians limped, their bodies wounded, but they refused to slow their advance.

"You have been warned!" the closest golem bellowed, the metal giant's voice filled with fury.

"Wait, here it is . . . here it is!" Planter held out the Amulet of Planes. The gem at the center burned with crimson intensity, forcing the two NPCs to shield their eyes.

Instantly, the iron golems stopped their advance and bowed their heads.

"You are welcome into the Hall of Planes," one guardian said, its voice deep and rumbly, like distant thunder.

Watcher sighed with relief and put a hand on Planter's shoulder. She turned and smiled back, and it seemed as if all his problems just evaporated. Glancing to the stairway, he signaled the rest to come out. Cautiously, the warriors emerged from the dark passage, their wary eyes still focused on the golems.

"By the looks of these golems, I have no doubt Krael and the Broken Eight came through here." Watcher pointed to the wounded guardians.

"Did you notice the pieces of iron on the ground?" Mapper said. "It seems as if the zombies and wither destroyed one of them."

Watcher nodded.

"Which portal do you think they used?" Planter asked as she put the Amulet of Planes back under her shirt.

"I can just barely see their charred footprints on the bedrock." Watcher knelt, allowing the Guardians of the Hall to see Er-Lan standing behind him.

"A warlock!" one of the metallic creatures roared. "These are not friends! ATTACK!"

"No, he's a friend! Er-Lan's a friend!" Watcher tried to explain, but by then the golem was within arm's reach; the metallic giant swung its muscular fists through the air, just missing him.

Rolling to the side, Watcher drew Needle and

crouched, ready to evade another attack. "Everyone, stay away from them!"

Some of the villagers drew bows and fired at the golems, but their arrows just pinged off their metal skin, doing no damage. One of the villagers drew a pick-axe and attacked, the metal tool denting the monster's chest, but then the golem raised its arms quickly, catching the NPC under the chin. The blow threw the warrior high into the air, flashing red as he took damage. Other villagers backed away from the golem, hoping to catch their comrade and limit his damage, but the doomed NPC flew sideways and sailed off the bedrock path, falling into the darkness. His screams continued as he fell; they seemed to go on forever.

More of the golems were drawing near, driving the NPCs back toward the stairway up to the surface.

"There is a charred footprint on one of the portals." Er-Lan pointed to the third glowing doorway. "The wither and Broken Eight went through that one. That is the path to follow."

"Right . . . everyone get behind me." Watcher put away his sword and drew the Flail of Regrets.

The enchanted weapon grew bright as power from Watcher flowed into the weapon.

"Stand back, I don't want to hurt any of you." He swung the Flail over his head. "I'm a wizard and I command you to back up."

The iron golems just moved closer.

"Please! I don't want to hurt any of you." Just then, Watcher's arms flared bright, filled with magical power.

The guardians continued their advance.

"Everyone get ready." And then Watcher charged. "Follow me!"

He swung the Flail into the chest of the closest golem, knocking him to the ground, and ran toward the portal. As the metal monster struggled to stand, the rest of the villagers trampled over him, trying to keep up with Watcher.

A pair of iron fists streaked past his head. Watcher rolled across the ground, then swung the Flail at the golem's legs. The weapon smashed into the two steel pillars with a sickening crunch, taking the legs out from under the guardian. The huge creature crashed to the ground, the impact making the Hall of Planes shake.

Now, only one more guardian barred their path to the portal through which the wither and zombies had passed, the other golems too far away to be of any help.

Watcher held the Flail of Regrets before him, ready to attack. "I don't want to hurt you, but one way or another, you must let us pass. The wither and zombies are heading for the Cave of Slumber to release the wither army. We're going to stop them. Now, please, stand aside. I don't want to hurt you."

The golem glanced at its two fallen comrades, the metal beasts still struggling to get back to their feet, then glanced back to Watcher's glowing arms. The creature seemed to relax a bit, but when its metallic eyes fell upon Er-Lan, the golem stiffened again and stood tall. "Warlocks may not pass, and friends of warlocks may not pass."

Then, before Watcher could react, the Guardian of the Hall clenched a fist and swung at him, aiming directly for his head.

Fear seemed to envelop every fiber of his being. His arms still pulsed with power, but terror ruled his mind, making it impossible to think or move. But before Watcher could make himself duck or get out of the way, Planter leaped in front of him, her enchanted red shield held high.

The golem's fist crashed into the shield, causing the rectangle of wood and metal to flare bright, blazing with magical energy as purple flames covered its surface, pushing the giant back a step.

"Everyone, get into the portal," Planter shouted.

The golem attacked again, this time bringing both fists down toward Planter, who held the shield bravely over her head, hoping to deflect some of the damage.

Watcher cringed as he watched the scene play out as if it were in slow motion. He swung the Flail over his head, hoping to strike at the metal monster's arms, but they were too fast. His Flail missed.

The iron fists smashed down upon the shield, but, as before, the rectangle flared with magical power, creating a dome of flames that covered both Watcher and Planter and pushed the golem backward a couple of steps. Planter advanced, holding her shield tight in her hands.

"Everyone . . . go!" she shouted.

The other villagers ran over the fallen guardians, then stepped up to the shimmering portal with a single, charred footstep on its edge. They stood before the sparkling field, uncertain.

"All must hurry before additional guardians arrive," Er-Lan warned, pointing at the infinitely long hallway. More of the iron golems were coming; they would reach the group in minutes. "Quick, into the portal." The zombie glanced reassuringly at his companions as, with confidence on his scarred face, he stepped through the portal.

"Come on, everyone." Blaster jumped through the shimmering emerald field, disappearing from sight.

"Planter, Watcher, come on . . . into the portal." Cutter pushed a group of villagers through the portal, then dove through himself.

The rest of their company dove through the magical doorway, leaving Planter and Watcher alone with the golems.

"Walk backward toward the portal," Watcher told Planter as he held onto the back of her enchanted chain mail and guided her to the portal.

"Look out!" She held her shield up high as another metal fist came pounding down toward them.

The wooden rectangle of her shield flared bright again, filling the Hall with iridescent light and pushing the golem back three steps, where it crashed into the incoming guardians, causing them to stumble and fall to the ground.

"Hurry . . . run!" Planter turned and sprinted to the portal, then dove through.

Watcher glanced at the damaged golems, thinking with a shudder about the poor NPC who fell into the dark abyss wrapped around the Hall of Planes.

Then he dove through the portal, heading toward who knew what.

CHAPTER 10

Watcher tumbled through the portal and landed on a soft, spongy, pinkish-gray surface. Tiny black spores floated up from the ground, some of them getting caught in his nose and making him sneeze.

Sitting up, he looked around and found the NPC warriors in a defensive formation around the iron-ringed portal, each person holding an iron or stone pickaxe as they all stared at the magical green doorway with trepidation, as if expecting the iron golems to emerge at any second.

Standing, Watcher moved to Planter's side and helped her to her feet. He glanced at her shield, the purple flames that had saved them from the iron fists now extinguished.

Why didn't I know that shield could do that? Watcher pondered. *My magical powers must have leaked into it somehow.*

Planter put the shield back into her inventory, a strange expression on her face, as if she'd just been caught in a lie . . . somehow.

"Planter are you okay? You look—" Before he could finish, he was interrupted.

"Watcher, are you okay?" Fencer came running up and grabbed his arm with both hands.

"Yes, *we* are both okay . . . thanks for asking." Planter scowled at the young girl, then stormed away.

"You did it, Watcher, you stopped those terrible metal monsters." Fencer looked up at him as if he were a hero, which made him feel good.

Maybe I did do something pretty incredible back there, he thought with pride.

"Those weren't monsters, Fencer," Watcher said. "They were iron golems, and they're just doing what they are supposed to do: guard the Hall of Planes." Watcher glanced at the portal, the sparkling green field within its iron border almost beautiful to watch. "I don't think the golems are gonna come after us through the portals. They're likely only allowed to exist within the Hall of Planes."

"Good . . . they didn't seem all that friendly." Blaster smiled at him, then glanced at Fencer's hands on Watcher's arm.

Watcher looked at the girl, then pulled his arm free from her grip and moved toward the other warriors. "We need to get moving. Their tracks are easily visible on the ground." He pointed at the charred footprints on the pink mycelium blocks. They led across the landscape, heading to the north.

For the first time, Watcher looked at the terrain around them. They were on a huge mushroom island, with red and white mooshrooms walking in random directions. The brightly-spotted cattle with the tiny red and white mushrooms growing out of the top of their heads and backs walked toward Er-Lan. The zombie held his green hand out to the animals to pet them on their noses; he had a way with animals few understood. All across the pinkish-gray ground, little mushroom spores puffed upward, floating into the air for a bit, then settling back onto the blocky surface. Nearby, tall mushrooms stood upon the hills, some domed and spotted red and white like the mooshrooms, others a light brown and completely flat. The entire company could have easily gathered beneath one of the flattened mushrooms without feeling crowded. Each type stood on a striped white stalk, the huge structures gently swaying in the constant breeze.

Watcher turned to Mapper. "Any idea where we are, or what's up ahead?" He moved to the old man's side. "I'd like to know what we're heading toward, rather than just blindly following the zombie tracks."

"Well . . . I do have an idea." The old man gave a mischievous smile, then reached into his inventory and pulled out a map, its edges jagged and torn, as if it had been ripped from something larger. "Remember when we went into the map room a few months ago, in that forest mansion?"

· "You mean when we fought the vindicators and evokers on the way to the spider warlord's lair?" Watcher asked.

The old man nodded. "I remembered that the map spread across the table reacted to your touch and changed, showing us the terrain around the spiders' lair. Well . . . I thought having a portion of that map might be helpful, so I cut a piece off." He held the map up in the air, a satisfied grin on his face. "Here it is. I'm hoping it will show us what we need to know."

"I don't understand," Cutter said. "That piece of paper looks blank."

"Exactly." Mapper nodded his head. "But let's see what happens when Watcher holds it."

The old NPC held out the map to Watcher.

I hope my magic is strong enough for this to work, Watcher thought, reaching out to take it.

When he touched the map, there was a brief spark, then lines and scribbles appeared.

"Well look at that," Builder said. "It changed when he touched it." He moved closer to Watcher. "My little niece would love to see something like that."

Watcher smiled with pride as the soldiers murmured to each other, impressed.

"Let's see what it shows." Mapper scanned the map from over Watcher's shoulder.

The map showed their position at the center of the mushroom island. Around them were various biomes, some of which Watcher couldn't discern from the map, though others were obvious: deserts, forest, grasslands . . .

Pinch the map . . . A familiar voice whispered into the back of Watcher's mind. Reaching into his inventory, he lifted out the Flail of Regrets and held it by his side, the large, spiked cube resting on the ground.

What? he thought to the mysterious presence existing within the magical weapon.

Pinch the map to see beyond.

Beyond? And then he understood.

Watcher put two fingers on the map, then slid them together, as if he were pinching the surface of the map. Instantly, the image compressed as if it had just zoomed out, showing a larger part of the landscape.

"What just happened?" Mapper asked.

"I just zoomed out a bit."

"How did you know to do that?" the old man asked, amazed.

"Well . . . it's a wizard thing." Watcher sounded pleased with himself and smiled, but then frowned when he saw Planter and Blaster both roll their eyes. "What . . . ?"

They just shook their heads.

Seek the Compass, the ancient voice whispered into Watcher's mind.

He scanned the map and instantly found a shape that looked like a compass. It was a circular structure with four sharp points pointing to the North, South, East, and West. Watcher pointed at the object.

"That's where we must go . . . to the Compass. I think we'll find the location of the Cave of Slumber there." Watcher glanced to the sky and checked the flow of the clouds to identify which way was north-east, then pointed in that direction. "We need to go that way."

"How can you be so sure?" Cutter asked, an accusatory tone to his voice.

"Well," he glanced down at the Flail still in his hand, then brought his gaze back to the big warrior. "I just know, and that should be good enough for all of you."

"I believe you." Fencer stepped forward and moved to Watcher's side. "I'm sure you know what you're doing. You are a wizard, after all."

More eyes rolled as Watcher nodded. He felt the rest of the company staring at him with disapproving glares. It made him feel as if he were somehow different from them . . . and he was.

None of them understand the responsibility that comes with these magical powers, he thought. *I'm always expected to save the day and use some enchanted thing to defeat the monsters. None of them really understand or care, except for . . .*

He glanced at Planter, who was scowling at him. But just then, Fencer stepped in front of him and gave Watcher a warm smile.

"You think we should get moving now?" the young girl asked.

"Oh, yeah, Fencer's right. We should get moving." He glanced up at the sun, and, for the first time, he noticed its color was . . . wrong. Instead of being a warm, rich yellow, the sun looked as if the color had been leached out of it, leaving a pale, sickly yellow that was harsh to the eyes. The glowing square was approaching the western horizon. "It looks like we don't have much time before nightfall. Everyone, follow me."

He headed off across the pinkish-gray landscape toward the north-east, weaving around the bright red mooshrooms as he walked. Glancing over his shoulder, he watched as the rest of the party reluctantly followed, many of them grumbling under their breath.

"Don't worry, Watcher, I'm sure you'll find this cave of yours," Fencer said, delighted to be walking next to him.

"Yeah . . . right," Watcher replied, feeling uncertain for some reason.

He could feel Planter's stare burning into the back of his head, but he didn't dare look back; he wasn't sure if he could face her anger right now. So instead, he just marched across the mushroom island, heading for the mysterious Compass in the distance, the footprints of the Broken Eight going in almost the same direction, but not quite.

It'll be good to get away from those terrible footprints for a change, Watcher thought.

They will return, the Flail murmured in his mind. *The Eight always return.*

And those words drove icy daggers of fear into Watcher's soul.

CHAPTER 11

Krael floated high in the air, his ashen bones merging with the pitch-black night sky, making him almost invisible, with only the stars being blocked out by his dark body and the two glowing crowns on his skulls making his presence known. Below, the Broken Eight walked with their direwolves at their sides, the octet anxious to begin their retribution.

Around them, unnaturally tall spruce trees stretched up into the air, the dark branches looming high overhead almost lost in the gloom of the night. Unseen creatures flitted about between the branches, squeaking with annoyance, their red, beady eyes staring down at the intruders with caution.

"Wither, where are you leading us?" Ya-Sik shouted into the night.

The king of the withers slowly descended to the ground, moving just close enough to the zombies that the shimmering purple light from their enchanted armor bathed him in an iridescent glow. But he still stayed out of reach of their razor-sharp swords; Krael was no fool. He wove his way around a thick tree trunk, then spoke to his comrades. "We are heading toward the Cave of Slumber."

"This zombie doesn't see a cave," Tu-Sik said. "Where is this cave?"

"I will find it soon enough." Center's voice had an irritated edge.

"How dare that zombie question us like that?" Left hissed quietly, seething with anger.

"Be quiet," Center whispered. "Say nothing to anger these zombies. I will deal with them in my own way and in my own time."

Krael smiled deviously, then moved closer to the zombies.

"How is it the king of the withers knows where it is located in this world?" Pe-Sik asked, his helmet in the shape of an evoker's head staring out into the empty night.

"We were here when it happened," Left said in a harsh, dismissive voice.

"That's right. We barely escaped when the wizards captured the other withers." Right's voice, as always, was calm and melodic. "If it weren't for our incredible skill in battle and careful plans, we'd be trapped in the Cave of Slumber right now with all the rest of the withers."

"No other withers are free?" Ur-Sik asked, the legs on his spider helmet brushing against the rough bark of a spruce, making a spooky scraping sound.

All three skulls shook their heads. "A few were scattered here and there, escaping the trap, but very few. The only way a wither can exist now is if they are summoned using souls and wither skulls. And usually, those that are summoned into existence are attacked and destroyed. None survive long."

"Then if Krael has been here before, then the wither is heading straight for the Cave of Slumber?" Ya-Sik asked.

"Well . . . it was hundreds of years ago." Krael floated higher into the air, out of reach of the zombies' swords. "We don't remember *exactly* where it is."

Some of the zombies growled. The direwolves sensed their anger and growled as well, each baring their sharp white teeth.

"But we remember some things," Right added quickly. "We know the Cave is in the Northern part of the world here, on the other side of the Creeper's Teeth."

"Creeper's Teeth?" two zombies asked at the same time.

"You don't know about the Creeper's Teeth?" Left jeered. "You zombies know nothing."

"Left, be quiet!" Center snapped.

"Tell us of the Creeper's Teeth." Ya-Sik demanded, glaring up at the wither king, the eyes on his dragon's head-shaped helmet glowing with magical energy.

"The Creeper's Teeth is a range of mountains formed by the wizards after they captured the withers." Center's eyes glowed with anger as he thought of his hated enemies. "They're steep mountains that reach high into the air, with their tops flattened, as if they couldn't grow any higher. Caves and tunnels pierce the sides of the peaks, with unnatural creatures waiting to attack anyone foolish enough to climb them."

Krael descended closer to the zombies and lowered his voice.

"The wizards made the Teeth to keep anyone from reaching the Cave of Slumber, for the monsters on those peaks are vicious and powerful. Only the Broken Eight could get past them."

Ya-Sik and the other zombies smiled.

"While the Eight climb the Creeper's Teeth, I will be flying overhead, blasting the monsters with my flaming skulls, keeping all of you safe. But if any monster sneaks past my barrage, your swords and direwolves will be enough to destroy them."

"If Krael can fly over the Creeper's Teeth, why are the Broken Eight needed?" one of the zombies asked, doubtful.

"First of all, I could not have made it past the

Guardians of the Hall without your blades and wolves."
Krael bowed his head to the zombies, thanking them
for their ferocious fighting. The zombies stood tall with
pride. "Second, the magic used to make the Broken
Eight will help me to cancel out the enchantments in
the Cave of Slumber. Without the Broken Eight, I would
become susceptible to the Cave's magic, and might
never escape. But with the eight of you, we will be able to
release my wither companions, then exact our revenge
upon the Far Lands and all of its inhabitants."

The zombies nodded, pleased with the last part.

"So, the wither king's plan is to walk around until
luck happens to lead to the Cave of Slumber?" Ya-Sik's
question had an accusatory tone.

"When I get near, I will feel the pull of its magic,"
Krael said. "The enchantments in the Cave of Slumber
were made to draw withers to it, then ensnare them in
the shadowy cavern. When we are near, I will know it."
The center skull smiled. "That's when the fun will begin.
But until then . . . we search."

They moved through the forest, passing the gargantuan trees in complete silence, both the zombies and
the wither king lost in thoughts of violence and revenge.
As they continued to the north, toward the distant and
unseen Creeper's Teeth, sounds of life started to become
audible from the treetops. Torchlight flickered between
the branches, making it clear something was up there.

Krael chuckled as he gazed upward. "There is a village overhead."

The zombies stared up at the warm glow leaking
through the foliage.

"This was the first community to rebel during the
Great War," the wither king said. "I think we will do
an experiment with them. You'll enjoy this." He glared
down at the zombies. "Do not destroy them unless I give
the word."

The zombies all nodded.

Up ahead, a spiral staircase wrapped around the

trunk of one of the larger trees. The zombies moved up the stairs, their golden armor clanking against the tree's bark, the direwolves following silently behind. Krael floated upward, following the progress of the zombies as they moved higher and higher up the tree.

When they passed through the lowest branches, they found wooden homes built within the treetops. Narrow walkways spanned the open air between trees, connecting clusters of homes with each other. Standing amongst the homes were villagers, zombies, skeletons, and endermen. Each wore clothing of brown-and-green cloth woven from fibers supplied by the forest, even the monsters. Their clothing almost blended in with the leafy background.

"What kind of foolishness is this?" Ya-Sik growled quietly. "Villagers and monsters living together . . . it is obscene."

"Be patient, my friend," Krael said. "Let's have some fun. Here's what I want you to do." The wither whispered in the zombie leader's ear, and all the while the monster nodded. When he was done, Ya-Sik smiled.

The king of the withers floated toward the largest collection of individuals, while the Broken Eight and direwolves moved toward a collection of zombies and skeletons.

"Hello, strangers." A villager in a dark-brown smock with a green stripe running down the center stepped forward. "We haven't seen any new villagers or monsters for a long time, but all are welcome in this community. What brings you to our trees?"

"What brings us here?" Krael asked, as if the question were ridiculous. "Why, the Great War, of course."

"The Great War?" The villager laughed. "That has been over for hundreds of years. On this plane of existence, villagers and monsters live together in peace. We are all equal here."

"Equal? Ha! You still call them monsters. That doesn't sound very equal to me." Krael floated over to the village leader and gently pushed him away from the monsters, then lowered his voice and whispered to the NPC. "The war is not over."

The villager looked stunned.

Krael nodded. "I'm here escorting these zombies to prison for their crimes; they've been sentenced to life in the Cave of Slumber. Right now, they obey my commands, but I don't know how long the enchantments put onto them will last." He moved closer to the NPC. "Rebellion is sweeping the land, with monsters rising up and attacking villagers. There is hate brewing between the races."

"That's impossible," the villager objected. "Racism and hate is something that is learned, passed on from parent to child. Here, parents teach about peace to all children, both villager and monster alike. We all work together to create a society better than the one that led to the Great War."

"Well, I have news for you, friend," Krael said, the lie flowing from his mouth with ease. "Zombies and skeletons and endermen have killed villagers in their sleep all across the land. They're taking over, just as they tried to do before the Great War. In fact, there's a wizard in this land ready to reignite the fires of war. He's telling all NPCs to gather their weapons and imprison all the monsters they see."

"I don't believe it. Our monsters are peaceful." The villager shook his head.

"You just said 'our monsters' as if you owned them." Krael shook his head as if disappointed. "Doesn't sound very equal to me. How do you think the zombies, skeletons, and endermen feel about you referring to them as your property, that they're monsters instead of equals?" He lowered his voice to but a whisper. "I suspect resentment has been growing amongst them for quite a while. Look at them."

On the other side of the treetop, Ya-Sik was talking to the monsters, giving a similar speech, but beyond the hearing of the villagers. The zombies and skeletons were frowning, some of them snarling toward the villagers. They glanced at their woven smocks, clothing exactly like what the villagers were wearing, and frowned. Some removed the garments, tearing them from their bodies.

"You see . . . already, their anger is growing." Krael turned and looked at the other villagers gathered around him. They all wore similar coarsely woven green-and-brown smocks. "I ordered my zombies to calm your monsters, but it's not working. Their rage has been growing for a long time. I've seen the same in other villages, and the end result is always the same."

The king of the withers grew quiet and moved to a dark part of the treetop, the enchantments from the dual Crown of Skulls on his two heads bathing him in a soft purple glow. He smiled as the villagers whispered to each other, some running to their homes for weapons and armor.

"Perhaps warning the other villages of this threat would be a good idea," Krael said to the leader.

The villager nodded nervously and glanced at two NPCs. They took off across the treetops, heading for other communities with the warning.

"I'm not convinced *our* community is in any danger," the village leader said. "We are a peaceful village."

"You're right, this is a peaceful village," Krael said. "That is, until it isn't anymore. I pity the parent who waits until it is too late to protect their children. I've seen it too many times, but maybe you're right; maybe it won't happen to you." All three of Krael's skulls shook their heads sadly. "It'll be unfortunate if you're wrong."

"Not just unfortunate," Right said. "It'll be fatal to all those kids."

The three wither skulls lowered their gaze to the leafy rooftop below, as if praying. Slowly, Krael drifted back to the steps, then motioned for the zombies to follow him. The Broken Eight moved away from the group of monsters, who were now frothing with anger.

"Time for us to leave, but first, we need to light the fuse." Center smiled at Ya-Sik. "Send one of your dire-wolves around behind the villagers and have it destroy someone. Make sure the villager has time to yell out before they're destroyed. Then return here, unseen."

The zombie nodded, then knelt next to his direwolf and whispered into the creature's ear. The monster bared its teeth, then took off, silently loping through the darkness like the shadow of a ghost. Moments later, a scream pierced the forest roof, then grew silent.

"Something killed Woodcutter!" an NPC shouted.

"I bet it was the zombies!" another yelled.

At the sound of the voices, the village's zombies growled, slowly extending their claws. Nearby, skele-tons notched arrows to bows as they formed ranks.

Watching it all happen, Krael smiled. "I guess the vil-lage leader was right; racism and hatred are learned . . . and we just gave them their first lesson." He laughed. "I'm sure they'll do the rest of the teaching themselves."

The Broken Eight smiled, some chuckling.

Suddenly, the village monsters charged at the NPC villagers, just as they were emerging from their homes with swords and shields in hand. The clashing of iron against claws rang out across the treetops, the *woosh-ing* of endermen adding to the sounds of battle.

"You see, Ya-Sik, it's much more satisfying to cause these fools to destroy themselves than it is to do it our-selves." He smiled down at the zombie leader, then floated down the spiral staircase. "Likely, those runners will start the same fires of hatred in the other villages. This will be fun to watch."

"The king of the withers has taught the Broken Eight a great lesson," Ya-Sik said, grinning. "Causing destruction through others can be more fun than doing it personally."

"Now you're learning, Ya-Sik. Now you're learning." Krael nodded. "And I still have so much to teach you. We'll cause great destruction together, you and I."

The zombie leader nodded as he descended the staircase.

"Come, let us continue our journey," Krael said. "Who knows how many other communities we can destroy with just a few words? But when we get to the ground, I want three of your zombies to head to the north-east. There is a structure called the Compass. I'm sure our friends will be there soon, and I'd like your zombies to give them a little greeting."

"That can be arranged." Ya-Sik gave the wither a toothy smile.

He pointed at three of the zombies. They descended quickly down the stairs with their direwolves following. When they reached the ground, they took off to the north-east while the rest of the party headed north toward the Creeper's Teeth.

CHAPTER 12

Watcher moved through the landscape, amazed at what he was seeing. Oaks and pines and birch trees filled this forest, dotting the rolling hills with their tall magnificence, but there was something obviously different here. The trees were all bent and crooked, like the acacia trees of the savannah, but they weren't in the savannah; they were in what seemed to be a typical forest biome. Somehow, the characteristics of the acacia trees had been transferred to the oaks, pines, and birches, making the entire forest feel as if it were moving, squirming to some unheard melody, and then frozen in place. It was both fantastic to see and disturbing at the same time.

The sun's harsh, pale face slowly emerged from behind the eastern horizon. Muted tones of red and orange washed across the sky, but there was a richness missing from it, as if much of the color had been sucked from the sky, just as it had been from the sun. The normally vibrant show in the sky was muted and pale and added a depressing feel to the environment. Somehow, this land, including even the sun, had been wounded in the past, and it still suffered.

"This is the strangest place I've ever seen," Mapper said softly. "Even the shrubs seem distorted."

The old man pointed to a cluster of plants. Instead of being a small pile of leaves, the blocks swirled upward in a spiral shape, slightly bent to the side, as if the wind were knocking them over.

"I don't think I like this place." Planter pulled out her enchanted bow. "It gives me the creeps."

"It doesn't bother me." Fencer skipped along and caught up to Watcher, then matched him step for step. "I bet Watcher could put it back to the way it should be if he wanted to, couldn't you?"

"Well, I don't know about that." Watcher glanced at the young girl. She had such an expression of complete confidence that it made him feel . . . well . . . good inside. It was as if she *really* believed in him.

Glancing over his shoulder, he saw countless NPCs rolling their eyes at the young girl's comments. Fencer moved closer to him, forcing Watcher to try to move away and almost causing him to collide with a twisted and contorted birch tree. Watcher heard Blaster giggle and glared at him. The boy just smiled back at Watcher, apparently entertained by his predicament.

"Looks like there's a village ahead," Planter said, her voice sounding annoyed.

"I think we should go check it out." Blaster put his dark green helmet on his head and dashed past Watcher and Fencer, still giggling.

Planter zoomed past them without a glance; no laughter was coming from her.

Watcher sighed as he watched Planter run with Blaster toward the village. *She should be running with me,* he thought, then glanced at Fencer. She gave him a huge grin, her confidence in him evident, as always, on her face. He knew he had to say something to Fencer, but it would crush the young girl, and he didn't want to hurt her. *Maybe if I just ignore her, she'll go away, and then I can be with Planter again, without all this stress,* he thought.

Reaching down to his chest plate, Watcher adjusted his enchanted diamond armor, then ran after his friends, the rest of the army following suit behind him. He wove around trees and past shrubs, trying to put the plants between him and Fencer.

Slowly, the wooden buildings of the village emerged from between the distorted trees. Watcher expected it to look like any other village, but was surprised when he got a good look at the structures. Like the forest, the buildings were warped and deformed, with walls sloped into bizarre shapes and roofs pitched at strange angles. It was as if a child had molded the homes out of clay, then pushed on the creations in random ways, leaving the village as misshapen as the trees that bordered the community.

Watcher could feel the tension in their company. More NPCs drew weapons and shields as the strangeness of the village became clear.

"What do you think the villagers will look like?" one of the soldiers asked hesitantly.

"I hope they aren't as warped as their houses," another said, sounding nervous.

Watcher nodded . . . he hoped the same thing as well.

Up ahead, Planter and Blaster were at the center of the village, standing near the community's well; the normally square structure was squashed and warped on one side. Stone bricks lined the courtyard; some of them cracked, while green moss covered others. Along the edges of the square, torches atop fenceposts flickered, still burning from the previous night. Homes of every shape and size bordered the square, their doors and windows facing the gathering place. Slowly, Watcher and the other NPCs gathered around the well, watching in all directions for the inhabitants to emerge.

The moo of a cow floated out from the animal pens

nearby, followed by the clucks of chickens and the bleating of sheep. Torches flickered into life within the bizarrely shaped wooden homes as the village slowly woke from its evening nap.

An NPC stepped out of a home and spotted the visitors, then quickly ran off.

Watcher sighed. "The NPC looked normal." He glanced at his companions. "Fortunately, he wasn't distorted or twisted like the village or forest."

Many of the warriors lowered their weapons and relaxed; the expectation of mutant villagers charging out of their homes now thankfully erased.

A group of villagers stepped out from a large structure that was twisted and bent to the side. The NPC at the front of the welcoming committee was old, with long gray hair that hung down past his shoulders. He wore a white smock with a gray stripe, marking him as the community's cleric, just like Watcher's father.

"Welcome, friends. You do not need your weapons here." The old villager and his companions held out their hands, showing they were unarmed.

Watcher glanced at Blaster and Cutter. They nodded and put away their weapons as Watcher and the rest of the NPCs did the same.

"I see you have a zombie with you," the village leader said.

"Yes, but you don't need to be alarmed." Watcher moved to the zombie's side. "This is Er-Lan, and he is our friend. You need not be afraid of him."

"Afraid? Why would we be afraid?" the villager said.

"Oh . . . well . . . great." Watcher felt surprised by their reaction, but happy too. Some reacted poorly to Er-Lan's presence; he was glad that wasn't the case in this village.

"My name is Cleric, and I am the leader of this community." The villager extended a hand to Cutter.

The big NPC shook hands with him, then glanced suspiciously at the other inhabitants of the warped village. They all stepped forward and shook hands with everyone in Watcher's company, making the group relax even more.

"We've never seen you in these parts," Cleric said. "Where are you heading?"

"Well, we're looking for the Compass." Watcher stepped forward and faced the old NPC. "But only have a vague idea where to go . . . north-east."

"That's correct," Cleric said. "Eventually, you'll run across a road made of stone-bricks. Many of the blocks are probably missing, but you'll still be able to see it if you—"

"Monsters approaching," Blaster warned, his voice loud enough for all to hear.

The group drew their weapons as a group of zombies, skeletons and endermen approached from another cluster of twisted homes. Gripping his sword firmly, Watcher glanced at the village leader. "Don't worry. There aren't very many of them. We can take care of them."

"What are you talking about?!" Cleric pushed Watcher's blade down, then grabbed Planter's bow and pointed it to the ground. He ran throughout the courtyard, trying to take weapons from the NPCs' hands, then finally moved toward the approaching monsters and stood in front of them, shielding the creatures with his own body. The monsters all had relaxed postures and pleasant smiles on their faces; they were not tense in any way. "These monsters live in our village. They are part of our community. Lower your weapons this instant!"

A scowl came across the old man's face, reminding Watcher of his own father. And then he noticed it: none of the zombies were extending their claws, none of the skeletons had fitted arrows to bowstrings, and the endermen's hands were not balled into fists. These creatures were not coming to fight.

"Everyone, lower your weapons." Watcher slowly put Needle back into his inventory, but kept a hand near it in case he needed to get to the enchanted blade quickly. "Sorry, I guess we're used to having monsters attack us."

"Well, that doesn't happen here!" Cleric snapped. "In this world, the cycle of violence that started in the Great War has been stopped. We teach our young, villager or monster, that all creatures are equal and should be treated with respect. Hate and racism are no longer passed down from parent to child; that type of behavior is forbidden."

The old man finally lowered his arms and slowly approached the group, while the monsters, still nervous, held their position on the other side of the courtyard.

"We're sorry," Planter said sincerely. "In our world, the monsters are always attacking villagers whenever they can."

"I don't think I like your world very much." Cleric shook his head as if he disapproved of all of them.

"Look, we aren't here to compare worlds." Blaster stepped up to the village leader. "We're here to find the Compass and stop the king of the withers. You already told us which way we need to go, so thanks and goodbye."

"Blaster . . . be nice," Planter chided.

"What? I'm just saying what we're all thinking." Blaster looked at his companions; many were nodding their heads. "We need to get moving before it gets—"

"More monsters coming in," Cutter whispered. "I don't have a good feeling about this."

A group of monsters, each clothed in greenish-brown garments, was approaching the village. Their clothing appeared to be woven from a thick, natural fiber Watcher had never seen before; it probably came from the trees, he guessed.

"Those are just monsters from the Treetop village," Cleric said. "Put down your weapons. All monsters are friendly here." He scowled disapprovingly at the newcomers, glaring at them until they put away their swords.

"Welcome, friends," Cleric said as he approached the monsters, but as they entered the square, they veered away from the NPC and headed for the other monsters.

"Everyone, get ready," Watcher whispered.

"What is it?" Planter asked.

"Look at their faces." Watcher gestured to the new monsters. "Those that just arrived don't have smiles and relaxed expressions on their faces. They're angry and looking for someone to pick on, or worse. I saw it hundreds of times from the bullies in the village."

"The new zombies have claws extended," Er-Lan said. "These monsters come for violence."

The newly arrived creatures stood amongst the rest of the monsters, whispering. They glanced at Cleric and the rest of the villagers, then went back to their discussions.

"Cleric, I think you had better come over here," Watcher said in a calm voice, trying not to give away his concern.

The monsters were raising their voices louder now. Some of the zombies snarled toward the villagers as more NPCs emerged from their homes and congregated in the square. At the same time, more monsters were emerging from their homes to see what was happening.

"Everyone, stay calm," Watcher whispered. "But keep your eyes open."

The monsters were now growling and becoming agitated. Watcher could see the creatures from the Treetop village were saying things to the other monsters, then pointing to the NPCs with clawed fingers. Some of the skeletons fitted arrows to bows.

"Cleric, I think you have a problem here," Blaster said.

"No, I think the problem is you and your friends," Cleric accused. "You came here with your weapons and suspicions, and now the monsters are getting upset."

"You see," one of the endermen said, pointing with a dark finger. "He calls you monsters, as if you're something unnatural. The villagers were never your friends; they're your masters, because you are allowing them to do this to you."

"What a minute." Cleric approached the monsters. "We have a peaceful community here, and talk like this will only—"

Before Cleric could finish his statement, the monsters attacked. A dozen arrows struck the old NPC, instantly destroying him. He disappeared from sight with a look of surprise on his wrinkled face.

"Monsters . . . attack!" one of the endermen screeched.

Watcher drew Needle from his inventory and charged toward the monsters. He could hear the thundering footsteps of Cutter on one side, Blaster on the other. Flaming arrows zipped over his shoulder as Planter opened fire.

Some of the village's NPC inhabitants tried to intervene and protect the monsters, but they were quickly destroyed by zombie claws.

"You don't get it!" Watcher screamed as he attacked one of the endermen, the lanky creature teleporting away. "The Great War has begun again. The monsters are a threat to you."

The enderman chuckled and disappeared, only to reappear right behind Watcher. The boy, sensing its presence, spun and slashed at the monster's legs, then lunged, scoring another hit before it could flee. The dark creature disappeared with a pop, leaving behind three balls of XP.

The other members of Watcher's company now stood shoulder to shoulder battling the monsters, the inhabitants of the village still trying to pull them away from the fighting. One of the NPC warriors, Builder, was injured, as a baker tried to keep him from attacking a skeleton with his sword. The skeleton's arrow found a gap between Builder's armored plates and struck the NPC in the shoulder.

"Everyone, back up," Watcher shouted.

The NPCs moved away from the monsters, stopping the battle for just a moment.

"You can't do this," one of the village leaders said. "These monsters are part of our community."

"Not anymore," Blaster said. "They're fighting the Great War, and you are their enemy, whether you like it or not."

"That's not true," the villager said defiantly. "All of you caused this violence by coming here. Now get out of our village . . . NOW!"

"You don't understand," Watcher said. "If we leave, then the monsters will destroy everyone in this village unless you fight back."

"And I bet you don't know how to do that," Cutter added.

"Do you have any weapons?" Planter asked.

"We don't need any weapons," the villager snapped. "Weapons only bring violence. Now get out of our village, before we throw you out."

More of the community's NPCs gathered together, their angry stares focused on Watcher and his friends, not the monsters. The biggest villagers stepped closer to Watcher and his friends, clearly threatening them. They had no weapons or armor, but seemed prepared to lift them off the ground and literally throw them from the village.

"Don't you understand? Something's changed with the monsters of this world." Watcher's eyes were pleading with the NPCs. "They are no longer your friends. The Great War is somehow reignited, and—"

Suddenly, the monsters charged, each one of them screaming their battle cry. The NPCs in the village held their hands out, showing they were unarmed, but the monsters just tore into them with their claws and fists and arrows. Many fell before Watcher and his companions could mount a defense.

Forming a battleline, Watcher and his companions pushed the monsters back. Archers on the flanks fired at skeletons as the swordsmen charged into the center.

Needle flashed through the air as Watcher dove into the battle. He could hear villagers behind him still objecting to the fighting, but their shouts turned to screams of pain as monsters slipped past the group's formation and found them. With Cutter's diamond blade on one side of him and Planter's golden axe on the other, Watcher crashed through the enemy, slaying many. Some monsters fled the village, taking their hate with them, but when Watcher eventually turned to check on the other NPCs, he found none standing. Piles of items and glowing balls of XP marked where the unarmed villagers had fallen to monster claws, leaving the community unnaturally quiet. Watcher turned in a circle, looking for any other living creatures, but there were none.

"It seems the Great War has begun anew," Mapper said gravely as he handed out potions of healing to the wounded in their company.

"Did we lose anyone?" Watcher asked, fearing the answer.

"Nope, everyone is accounted for," Fencer said. "You saved everyone."

Many of the NPCs grumbled in disbelief.

"Look around you, Fencer. You see all those balls of XP?" Planter was furious.

Fencer took a step back and nodded.

"Those used to be villagers, just like you and me. Now they're gone."

Fencer hung her head, tears trickling from her eyes.

"Planter, she didn't mean anything by it," Watcher said, then immediately regretted coming to her aid.

Planter flashed him a glare, then stormed off. "I'm checking the village for anything useful."

"That's a good idea," Mapper said, scurrying after her. "I bet there are some potions around here that might be handy to have. 'Have a potion for every occasion,' that's what I always say."

They searched the village and found neither weapons nor armor, but they were able to stock up on potions of healing, leaping, and regeneration, as well as a good supply of food. With their inventories bulging, they left the village in complete silence. It felt to Watcher as if they were leaving a crime scene.

And for some reason, he felt like the criminal.

CHAPTER 13

They walked through the twisted forest until noon, no one speaking a word. The incident at the village had been shocking, and though they had destroyed all the rebellious monsters, Watcher and all his companions regretted not saving the villagers. They all felt responsible, yet there seemed to be no way to help NPCs who wouldn't help themselves.

"I don't understand what Krael hopes to gain by rekindling the Great War." Watcher finally broke the silence, shaking his head as he tried to make sense of it.

"Maybe he hoped he could slow us down," Blaster said.

Planter shook her head. "No, he did this for one reason, and only one reason . . . because he could." She glanced at Watcher, then cast her gaze on Fencer, who was staring adoringly at the boy.

"We need to find that wither and stop him once and for all!" Blaster instinctively drew his curved knives, then realized he was the only one with weapons in hand and put them back into his inventory.

"Look, a brick path." Mapper ran ahead, then stopped and stared at the ground.

Watcher sprinted to his side and looked down. Stone

bricks were embedded into the ground, their surfaces cracked and worn from age. "This must be the path."

Mapper nodded, then checked the position of the sun. "I think we should hurry. Being in this twisted forest at night seems like a bad idea."

"Yeah, I agree," Watcher said, looking around. "Especially with the escalation of violence between monsters and villagers."

The rest of the NPCs gathered around Watcher and Mapper.

"Who do you think made this path?" Builder asked.

"Must have been constructed by the ancient wizards," Mapper said. He kicked at one of the bricks, causing part of the block to flake off and crumble to dust.

"They didn't do a very good job," Blaster said with a sarcastic smile. "It looks like it only lasted a couple of centuries." He laughed, lightening the mood for everyone.

"I'm sure Watcher could have built something better with his magical powers." Fencer's voice was filled with adulation. "His path would have lasted much longer than this one. After all, he is a great wizard, and . . ." she droned on, no one listening.

Planter glared at Watcher as if demanding him to do something, fury in her eyes.

What does she expect me to do? I can't make it so Fencer can't speak, Watcher thought. In response, he looked down at the ground.

Planter sighed, then pushed back the villagers and stood directly in front of Fencer.

"You know I'm standing right here, don't you?" she asked the young girl.

"Here it comes," Blaster said slowly, then backed away. Taking his cue, the other NPCs did the same, except for Watcher.

"What are you talking about?" Fencer asked.

"You're saying all these foolish things to Watcher, complimenting him on this and that. Don't you think

I know what you're trying to do?" Planter put her fists on her hips and glared at the girl. "You followed us all the way from our village in the Wizard's Tower just to be with him. And now I see you always chasing after him, trying to stand next to him, always brushing your hand against his and batting your eyes at him. I know what you're trying to do, and it isn't gonna work."

"Planter, I don't know what you're talking about," Fencer said. "I just think Watcher is awesome, and he can—"

"You see . . . there you go again!" Planter's face was beginning to turn red as her anger grew. "I won't stand for it . . . I won't."

Fencer now took a step back; she looked afraid of Planter.

This is getting out of control; I have to stop this, Watcher thought.

Moving between the girls, Watcher turned and faced Planter. "You know she doesn't mean anything. Fencer is just a kid, and I think she was genuinely concerned about me when she followed us from the Wizard's Tower."

Planter rolled her eyes.

Watcher reached out and grasped Planter's hand. "She doesn't mean anything. This is no big deal, trust me."

Planter's eyes narrowed as she glared at Watcher doubtfully. "I'm getting tired of this game Fencer's playing," she said in a low, venomous tone. "You better solve this problem, or I'm gonna solve it for you."

But before Watcher could answer, she yanked her hand from his, spun around, and walked down the stone path, with most of the villagers following. Watcher was left standing there, uncertain, with Fencer behind him. Blaster stood silently off to the side. When Watcher glanced at him, Blaster gave him a shrug.

"This girlfriend-thing looks like a bit of a challenge." His gaze flicked to Fencer, then back to Watcher, and he smiled. "Maybe getting an extra one wasn't such a good idea?" Blaster laughed, then ran off, chasing the others.

Fencer placed a hand on Watcher's shoulder. "Thank you for rescuing me. Planter scares me sometimes."

"I didn't rescue you!" Watcher snapped, then felt bad. "Sorry, I didn't mean to yell." He turned and faced her. "You have nothing to fear from Planter. My girlfriend would never do anything to hurt another person, so don't worry about it."

"You're the best." She smiled up at him with an almost reverent look in her eyes.

Watcher sighed and shook his head, then turned and chased the others, Fencer beside him. He never saw the six sets of eyes staring at him from behind a leafy hedge, half of them glowing red and all of them filled with hate.

CHAPTER 14

Planter led the company along the brick path, Watcher staying far to the rear. The trail led them through the twisted forest, curving around distorted trees and past strangely shaped pools of discolored water. The farther north they went, the more distorted the trees and plants became, until they barely resembled anything close to a tree or bush. Thick trunks of oak and spruce curved and bent until they folded back upon themselves, burrowing the treetops into the ground as if they'd been crushed. The distortion to the land seemed to get worse with every step.

"It's like a storm blew through here, warping everything it touched," Mapper said. "It makes me sad."

"Perhaps this was caused by the wizards," Er-Lan suggested. "Powerful magic was used to make the Cave of Slumber. That magic may have spilled over into these lands, destroying the natural rules of the Overworld." The zombie glanced back at Watcher. "No offense meant."

"None taken." Watcher smiled. "That was done a little before my time."

"I'd say," Cutter said. "About three hundred years before your time."

"Maybe more," Mapper added. "No one is really certain when the Great War happened. The only thing known for sure is it happened after what people call the Awakening."

"Look, the forest is ending." Planter pointed to the edge of the twisted forest biome.

Watcher moved up to Planter's side and stared out at the strange landscape. Before them, the ground sloped downward maybe twenty to thirty blocks, then extended in a massive recession. It seemed the land ahead of them had somehow sunken as if a giant had stepped on the rocky plane, causing it to sink below the level of the forest in which they stood.

Stranger still, there were huge arcs of stone stretched high into the air, forming gigantic gray half-circles. The curves were of all different sizes, from those bending eight blocks into the air to some extending upward twenty blocks or more. All of the bowed structures were aligned to the north as if drawn there by some gargantuan magnet, the constant east-to-west wind passing through the stony loops. Some of the arcs gave off a low hum, the wind pushing relentlessly against the granite structures, driving them like thick guitar strings. Watcher felt the ground vibrate ever so slightly. It felt like distant thunder, barely audible.

Beyond the strange, rocky structures was a huge wall of stone a dozen blocks high, if not more. It formed a curved barrier that wrapped around in a gigantic circle likely a hundred blocks in diameter. Within the center of the circle stood a lush forest, with green grass, tall oak trees dotted with bright apples, and the occasional pristine white birch tree mixed in.

Wide openings were carved into the massive wall, each one at the points of the compass: north, south, east and west. A line of tall oak trees bordered each side of the path leading into each of the entrances, the trees completely leafless, as if they were dead, but still standing. The sickly oaks made everyone a little sad, for just within the curved wall, the land was brimming with life, but outside everything was dead.

"Something terrible happened here." Er-Lan moved to Mapper's side and glanced at the old man. "The land is wounded."

"That seems to be a common theme in this world," Mapper said. "The Great War was not kind to this plane of existence."

"Are wars ever kind?" the zombie asked. "Hatred has a way of demanding a high price, yet giving nothing in return."

Mapper nodded. "What's that in the middle of the circular forest? I can't see any features; it's too dark."

Watcher took a few steps forward and stared out across the sunken landscape at the structure. At the very center of the perfect forest stood a tower made of midnight-black stone, totally out of place in the verdant woods. It looked to be more shadow than stone. Watcher instantly knew that it was their destination.

"I'm not sure what it is. It looks like it's more shadow than substance, but I think we found what we've been looking for." Watcher nodded and glanced around at his companions. "Everyone, welcome to the Compass. I have no doubt; we need to go to that tower at the center."

"You mean the one that looks like it's made of pure evil?" Blaster asked with a smile.

"Yep."

Blaster patted Watcher on the back sarcastically. "This *is* gonna be fun."

Without waiting for anyone to move, Blaster ran down the slope, heading for the strange rocky arcs, the rest of the party following behind him.

Watcher ran next to Er-Lan. The zombie was seemingly very disturbed by the place.

"You okay?"

The zombie nodded. "Many lives were lost in this place. Er-Lan can feel it."

They ran through the center of a small stone arc.

The ground vibrated from the hum of the structure, causing tiny bits of gravel and dust to dance about on the ground.

"Great and terrible magic spells were used here, devouring many; the appetite of war is likely still not satisfied." Er-Lan glanced at his friend. "By the looks of this world, much of it has been damaged by the magic of the wizards and warlocks."

"Yeah." Watcher nodded solemnly. "Fortunately, these battles of magic happened here and not in our Far Lands."

"Fortunate for Watcher's and Er-Lan's ancestors, perhaps," the zombie said. "But not very fortunate for those that lived here."

Watcher said nothing, the truth in his friend's words striking at him like a hammer. He was only thinking of *his* people, in *his* homeland of the Far Lands; he didn't consider all the people that probably suffered here. He felt ashamed.

They ran through a larger stone ring. The hum of the structure sounded like a deep growl from some ancient titanic beast; it made the ground shake, but also leaked into Watcher himself. He could feel his body vibrating with the thick, stony ring, as if he was becoming part of the structure; it was strange . . . and disturbing.

"There's the entrance!" Planter shouted, pointing to the line of dead oaks.

The trees were aligned right next to each other along the sides of the path with hardly any space between their trunks, creating a wooden wall. Planter pulled out her enchanted axe as she entered the woody passage. She glanced over her shoulder at Watcher, an expression of fear on her beautiful face. Watcher sprinted forward, reaching her side. He pulled out the Flail of Regrets and ran in lockstep with his girlfriend.

"Watcher, wait for me," Fencer shouted behind them.

Planter scowled, then sprinted ahead. At the same time, Blaster zipped past him, with Builder at the boy's side. They ran along the edges of the tree-lined avenue. But when they reached the entrance to the lush forest, they skidded to a stop, and Blaster drew his curved knives while Builder pulled out an iron sword and shield.

"The Eight," Er-Lan moaned. "The Eight are here."

Watcher glanced over his shoulder to his green friend, then raced to Blaster's side. Planter was already there, her axe held at the ready, the magical enchantments running through the weapon painting the ground with an iridescent purple glow.

"What's wrong?" Watcher asked. "Why'd you stop?"

Blaster glanced at him, then pointed with one of his knives.

Trees choked the green space within the curved walls, their snake-like roots crawling from the base of the oaks, then plunging into the dark soil. Between the oaks stood three zombies, each wearing magical gold armor, with helmets like the heads of different monsters: an enderman, an evoker, and a wolf.

Er-Lan moved next to Watcher and moaned with fear. "The Eight are here."

"I only see three of them." Watcher glanced at his friend. "Are there more here?"

"Three is enough for what they came to do," Er-Lan whimpered.

The rest of the party entered the edge of the pristine forest, their weapons drawn and ready. They completely outnumbered the three magical zombies, yet the trio of monsters seemed unconcerned. A sense of anger and vile malice surrounded each of the ancient zombies, their snarling faces were scarred from countless battles. The three monsters glared at Watcher, expressions of complete and absolute hatred on their terrifying faces.

"Let us pass and you will . . . not be harmed." Watcher tried to fill his voice with confidence, but it cracked with fear.

The zombie with a wolf helmet smiled a toothy grin, then drew a golden sword from his inventory and banged it against his shining chest plate, the metallic coating ringing like a gong. Instantly, a deep, growling sound filled the tree-lined passage behind the group. Glancing over his shoulder, Watcher spotted three gigantic wolves as they blocked the exit from the wooded passage, their fur bristling, their glowing red eyes filled with a thirst for violence.

"The wither king, Krael, sends his regards," the zombie warrior said, his voice, like the expression on the creature's face, full of hatred for their very existence. He pointed his razor-sharp sword at Watcher, then shouted a single word; it was deep-throated and guttural, as if growled by some ancient beast, the word filled with malevolence and a promise of pain:

"ATTACK!"

The zombies and direwolves charged, gold swords and sharp teeth gleaming under the afternoon sun.

CHAPTER 15

Watcher pulled the Flail of Regrets from his inventory and swung it over his head, putting every ounce of strength he had into the enchanted weapon. His arms glowed bright, the magic coursing through his veins flowing into the Flail and making it stronger. He ducked under one of the zombies' swords, then smashed the creature in the chest. Its enchanted golden armor made a sickening crunch as the spikes on the end of the Flail pierced the metallic coating and found soft flesh.

The creature screamed out in pain. Another zombie came to his aid, smashing into Watcher with a thick, curved shield. Sharp, pointed barbs across the shield's shimmering surface stabbed into Watcher's diamond armor, digging into the crystalline surface. Rolling across the ground, he swung his Flail at the creature's legs, knocking the monster to the ground.

A shout of pain pierced the forest, putting worry for his friends into Watcher's soul. Standing up, he backed away from the zombies and glanced toward the sounds. The huge direwolves were tearing into the NPC warriors, their sharp teeth shredding iron armor as if it were made of paper.

Putting the Flail back into his inventory, Watcher pulled out the Fossil Bow of Destruction, the enchanted weapon he'd taken from the skeleton warlord many months ago. Gritting his teeth and preparing for what was coming, he pulled back on the bowstring and aimed at the most vicious of the wolves. Instantly, an arrow appeared on the bowstring, and at the same time, pain surged through his body as the Bow used his HP to energize the powerful enchantments woven into the weapon.

Somehow, the wolves sensed the magical weapon instantly. They stopped their attack and stared straight at Watcher, their beady eyes glowing red with vicious anger. Chills of fear shuddered down his spine as the three animals loped across the grass-covered ground, snarling and baring their teeth.

Watcher released the arrow, his thoughts focused on his target. The arrow leaped off the bowstring and streaked through the air. The wolf saw the projectile and instantly curved to the left at the last instant, causing the arrow to miss, but the sparkling shaft arced around, tracking the target. The wolf, thinking it was safe, charged at Watcher, but before it could reach him, the arrow struck the animal in the side, instantly taking all of its HP. It yelped in pain, then disappeared, its snarling mouth still open as it tried to bite at Watcher. The other two wolves charged at their enemy. Watcher fell to one knee, his health low after using the bow.

Suddenly, Builder was at his side, throwing a potion of healing on the boy. The liquid seeped into Watcher's body, cooling the fiery agony that licked at his nerves. Standing, Watcher pulled the string back, getting ready to shoot, but he was too late; a direwolf jumped in the air and landed right on top of him, knocking him to the ground and sending the Bow of Destruction falling from his grip, out of reach.

Reaching into his inventory, Watcher pulled out a wooden shield and held it over him just in time as the creature snapped at his head. Its powerful jaws crashed together above him, sounding like a blacksmith's hammer banging against an anvil. Terrible odors came from the creature's mouth as it tried to bite at Watcher's face, the shield keeping the creature away, but just barely.

Suddenly, a scream pierced through the sounds of battle around them; it sounded as if a villager was grievously wounded. And then, out of nowhere, a glittering arrow struck the side of the wolf on top of Watcher, taking the vicious creature's HP to zero instantly. It disappeared with a look of surprise on its lupine face.

Another scream sliced through the air. Watcher set aside the shield and turned toward the sound. Builder was on one knee, his body flashing red. In his hand was the Fossil Bow of Destruction. The NPC drew the string back and fired an arrow at the last of the direwolves. The sparkling projectile hit the creature in the shoulder, causing it to disappear, a howl of pain just escaping its mouth before it vanished.

"Builder . . . no!" Watcher reached into his inventory and found a potion of healing. He threw it on the villager, but the liquid just bounced off him, the enchantment from the Bow likely canceling out the magic.

Builder flashed again, then fell to both knees weakly. He stared at the Bow of Destruction as if it were a deadly viper. He shook his hand, trying to dislodge the weapon, but it would not come loose from his grip.

Watcher ran to him and grabbed the bow. Pulling with all his strength, he tried to tear the enchanted weapon from the NPC's grip, but to no success. It was as if the weapon were a part of the NPC's body . . . for now.

"Here, Builder, eat something." Watcher handed him an apple.

The NPC tried to bite into the fruit, but it was magically pushed from his grasp as the Fossil Bow of Destruction punished the non-wizard for using the weapon.

"Someone . . . HELP!"

Watcher glanced around the battlefield, where Cutter and a handful of NPCs still fought with the first two zombie warriors. Nearby, Planter and Blaster battled with the third, Planter's golden axe crashing into the monster's armor while Blaster's curved knives slipped into gaps between the plates, making the creature flash red with damage, then disappear.

As the zombie vanished, Planter glanced in Watcher's direction, then came running, a golden apple in her hand. Kneeling at Builder's side, Watcher held the doomed villager's head in his lap, trying to comfort him as waves of agony crashed through the NPC.

"Builder, you saved me, but you shouldn't have used the Bow; it's only for wizards like me!" Watcher held his hand as another burst of pain spread through the villager's body.

With his strength waning, Builder shook the Bow again, still trying to dislodge it from his grasp, but Watcher knew it was futile. The villager finally surrendered to his fate and stared up at Watcher, fear and understanding in his brown eyes. Builder squeezed Watcher's hand feebly, then spoke, his voice barely a whisper.

"Protect my niece and nephew. You can do this, Watcher. You can defeat the wither king." Builder took a strained breath. "Just be true to your—"

And then he disappeared, leaving his items and the Fossil Bow of Destruction on the ground. Planter reached his side and stared down at the discarded inventory, a tiny square tear tumbling down her cheek.

"Oh no, Builder . . ." Planter moaned as she placed a hand on Watcher's shoulder.

Rage overwhelmed Watcher's mind as he stood. He picked up the Bow and stuffed it into his inventory, then pulled out the Flail of Regrets. His arms burned with enchanted power as his anger made them glow brighter and brighter. The magical power poured into the Flail, causing it to blaze with energy like a spiked, purple sun.

He rushed across the forest floor, swinging the Flail over his head, screaming his battle cry. He flung his weapon into the closest zombie warrior. The spiked ball crashed into the creature's chest plate, causing a wide crack to split down the middle. The monster moved his hand in shock across the fissure in his golden armor and screamed in rage, then attacked the wizard. Watcher ducked as the zombie's golden blade swung at his head, striking the trunk of a nearby tree. As the monster struggled to free his weapon from the wood, Watcher hit him again, knocking the enderman-shaped helmet from the creature's head. The zombie swung again at Watcher, but he'd already moved, rolling across the ground to the side. Standing, he brought the Flail of Regrets down upon the zombie with all his strength. The creature flashed red again and again, then disappeared, a sad moan escaping the monster's lips.

Before the last zombie could react, Watcher rushed forward to attack, but in his haste he tripped over one of the gnarled roots snaking across the forest floor. He fell hard, knocking the wind out of his chest. The zombie took that opportunity to slash at one more villager, then turned and fled. The gold-coated monster zigzagged between the trees as arrows sought to taste his HP, but they fell harmlessly to the ground. Some of the NPCs gave chase.

"Come back!" Watcher shouted to them as he stood. "We have more important things to do."

The villagers stopped their pursuit and returned to the others.

Watcher glanced at the ground. Discarded items lay strewn across the ground from fallen comrades. Guilt surged through his soul as he stared down at the glowing balls of XP.

The only thing marking these four NPCs' existence are

a few weapons, armor and glowing balls of XP, Watcher thought. *I failed them all.*

No, the ancient voice said deep within Watcher's mind; it was the Flail of Regret. *They left traces of themselves with all of you, through memories and stories and how they touched your hearts. They are never truly gone if you remember them.*

Watcher frowned, trying to force the tears to evaporate and just go away.

But Builder and the others suffered so much, Watcher thought.

He could still hear Builder's screams of pain and fear in his mind, echoing in his soul, forever reminding him of his failure, and regret.

Then remember them and honor their sacrifice, the Flail said, then grew silent.

Watcher looked up and realized his jaw was sore; he'd been gritting his teeth while he thought about Builder and the others. He heard sobs; Fencer was weeping, her arms wrapped around Mapper. Others looked sad, too, but their anger toward the Broken Eight and the wither king was so great, it pushed back the tears and replaced them with rage.

"The cost of this battle with just three of the Broken Eight was steep." Glancing around at the piles of tools and weapons, Watcher felt a tear trying to escape from the corner of his eye, but he refused to set it free. The time for grief was later; right now, it was time for action. "We must not let the sacrifices given here be in vain." He raised his hand into the air, fingers spread wide. "For Builder . . ."

"For Fisher . . ."

"For Carver . . ."

"For Saddler . . ."

The litany for the dead sounded hollow in this strange land, but Watcher knew their sacrifices had been important.

Clenching his hand into a fist, Watcher tried to

crush his sense of failure and regret at these losses, but he knew he'd done everything he could. Slowly, he lowered his hand, the others doing the same.

"We still must find the Cave of Slumber." Watcher pointed to the dark tower rising high over the forest. "Hopefully there will be some clues up ahead. Everyone, follow me."

After picking up all the items on the ground, they ran toward the dark structure looming above the forest, an uneasy silence spreading across the company. Watcher wove around the oaks and birches as they sprinted through the woods. The forest thinned as they grew nearer, then stopped completely, revealing a massive circle of quartz, the dark tower built at the center. Redstone blocks embedded in the pristine white surface outlined paths leading to the entrance of the tower.

The villagers stood at the edge of the quartz, unsure if it was safe to enter. Watcher glanced at Mapper, hoping for some indication from the old man on whether they should proceed. He was about to ask something when Planter appeared at his side.

"Do you hear it?" she asked.

"What?"

"Do you hear it?" Planter gave him an annoyed look.

"I don't know what you're talking about—" he began, and then he heard it. A high-pitched sound just at the edges of his perception hummed in lyrical tones, the harmonious notes soothing to his nerves. Watcher smiled and nodded. "Yes, I can hear it."

"Come on." Planter stepped onto the quartz circle, following the redstone-lined path.

Watcher looked up at the great tower as he followed Planter, trying to figure out what kind of blocks had been used in its construction. The dark cubes looked more like shadows than anything else; no purple speckles were visible, as he would expect if the blocks were obsidian; no black and gray colors, which he'd expect if they were bedrock. Even if they'd used blocks of coal, the edges where the cubes met would be visible, but the surface of the cylindrical tower was completely feature-less as it rose into the air, a mysterious anomaly.

When they entered the tower, Watcher found the inside lit with a complex pattern of redstone lanterns. They spiraled up along the inside of the tower all the way to the top, which was at least forty blocks into the air. They cast a warm yellow glow on the interior; it was a pleasant change from the harsh rays of this world's pale sun.

"It's coming from the center." Planter led Watcher toward the center of the tower, then knelt and listened, putting her ear to the ground.

"What are you doing?" Blaster asked.

"Shhh." She held a hand up into the air, silencing him.

Blaster glanced at Watcher and shrugged. Watcher put a finger to his lips and glanced at the other villag-ers, getting them to all stay quiet.

Planter moved from block to block, pressing her ear to the stone until she found the one she sought. Glancing up at Watcher, she smiled. "This one." She pointed at a specific block.

Watcher drew a pickaxe and swung it with all his might. After four hits, the quartz cube shattered, reveal-ing a wooden chest. Dropping his pick, Watcher knelt at Planter's side and slowly pried open the lid. The hinges squeaked loudly as it rose, causing rust to flake off the metal, creating a dusty cloud that made Watcher sneeze.

Inside the chest were two identical items; they looked like gauntlets that would attach onto someone's wrists, but each glowed with magical power. Planter reached for the items, but Watcher grabbed her hands.

"These could be dangerous, like the Bow of Destruction." He looked into her spectacular green eyes. "I don't want you getting hurt because of their enchant-ments. You better let me handle them for now."

She rolled her eyes, then moved back.

Watcher reached into the chest. When he touched the gauntlets, the magical relics jumped up and snapped around his wrist so suddenly it scared him. He leaped backward away from the chest, stumbled, then fell onto his back.

"You okay, Watcher?" Cutter asked.

The big NPC stood over him. He reached down and offered a hand to help the boy to his feet, but when he saw the magical gauntlets, he pulled back, uncertain about coming near the enchanted artifacts. Blaster moved to Cutter's side and stared down at Watcher.

"Whatcha doin' down there?" Blaster said. He glanced at Cutter, then turned back to Watcher and extended a hand, not caring about the gauntlets.

Reaching out, Watcher took the hand and let Blaster pull him to his feet.

"What are those on your wrists?" Cutter asked nervously.

"I don't know. They kinda just grabbed hold of me, and now they're there." Watcher tried to pull one off, but it didn't budge. "I don't think they're gonna let go, at least for now."

"That's tomorrow's problem," Blaster said. "Today's problem is finding the Cave of Slumber."

"I think I found it!" Mapper exclaimed. "Everyone come over here."

They moved to the old man. He was standing on the far side of the tower, where a large map covered the wall.

"It wasn't here before," Mapper said. "But when you opened that chest, it just appeared here." He pointed at a structure that looked like a compass. "That's us here. And then way up here is the Cave of Slumber."

"How do you know that's the Cave of Slumber?" Blaster asked from the back of the group.

"Well, I've read a lot of books about the ancient wizards," Mapper said. "I've looked at a lot of maps and studied the Great War for most of my life, so I should know. *Plus,* it says 'Cave of Slumber' in small writing." He smiled at Blaster.

"Ok then," the boy replied.

"What's that between us and the cave?" Watcher pointed to a zigzag line that cut all the way across the map from left to right. The tops of the zigzags were chopped off, leaving their peaks flat.

"Ahh . . . that's called the Creeper's Teeth." Mapper smiled with excitement. "I've read about them. The ancient wizards constructed the Teeth to keep villagers and monsters from some great treasure that lies to the north."

"And now we know what that treasure is." Planter pointed to the Cave of Slumber. "Obviously, the wizards wanted to keep everyone away from the army of withers imprisoned within the Cave."

"So we can just climb the Creeper's Teeth?" Cutter asked.

Mapper shook his head. "The books say the wizards covered the mountains with unimaginable monsters. Anyone trying to climb the Creeper's Teeth would face the worst horrors in Minecraft. With so few of us, I don't think we'd last very long."

"Then what are the alternatives?" Watcher moved closer to the map, surveying every inch. "What's this at the bottom of the mountains?"

Mapper moved up close. "The map has it labeled as the Labyrinth. I think it's a passage or tunnel that goes under the mountain. But its label has me a little concerned; it's written with some kind of dark-red ink."

Blaster moved up to the map and stared at the writing. "That doesn't look very inviting to me, especially written in red." He glanced at Watcher. "I think we should take our chances with the mountains."

Mapper shook his head. "Many will die if we go that way." His voice rang with certainty.

"I think we need to try the Labyrinth." Watcher glanced at Mapper. The old man nodded. "We'll have to just take a chance on what might be inside. My magical powers will protect us in the Labyrinth, I'm sure of it. The unknown will be better than a host of monsters waiting for us on the steep slopes of the Creeper's Teeth. We'll leave that problem for Krael and the rest of the Broken Eight."

"I hope you're right." Blaster stared at Watcher, a look of uncertainty in his brown eyes.

Watcher checked the map, then glanced up at the clouds overhead to get his bearings.

"OK, let's get moving," he said.

"But wait a minute." Planter put a hand on his shoulder. "Aren't you worried about those things on your wrists? You don't even know what they do."

"True, but I know their name." Watcher smiled, pleased with himself.

"Oh yeah? Then what are they called?"

"Well . . . they're the Gauntlets of Life." He held his arms in the air for all to see.

"How can you possibly know that?" Planter asked with a doubtful scowl.

"Because it says it right there." Watcher pointed to the side of each gauntlet. "Anything called the Gauntlet of Life can't be bad. Besides, if they are a problem, I'll just take care of them. Remember, I'm—"

"We know, you've told us a thousand times now," Blaster said. "You're a wizard."

Watcher smiled, pleased with himself again.

"And probably the best wizard ever," Fencer added with a grin.

Watcher's smile faded, but Blaster's spread as Watcher's discomfort with Fencer's adulation grew.

"Come on, everyone," Cutter said, his booming voice startling the rest of the villagers. "We have a labyrinth to go through, then some zombies and a wither to destroy. It won't get done if we stay here."

With a nod of agreement, Watcher took off running through the north exit of the tower, sprinting across the landscape toward whatever lay hidden in the dark passages of the Labyrinth.

CHAPTER 16

K rael smiled as the chaos spread through the village; the flames of rebellion lit by the king of the withers and the Broken Eight were doing their work. He floated away from the cliffside village and into the open air; far from the ground was his favorite place to be. He stared at the buildings and homes attached to the sheer side of the mountain, perplexed as to the purpose of this village. The NPCs had built their village on the vertical face of the cliff, their homes clinging to the wall as gravity tried to pull the unwary to the ground. From the other side, the mountain seemed like any other, but for some reason, the east side of the peak was completely missing. It was as if someone had sliced the mountain in half and took the eastern portion away as some kind of trophy. It made no sense to Krael.

They'd come to the village in the middle of the night. The Broken Eight, only five of them present at the time, had climbed the thin stairways zigzagging up the cliff face, rousing the monsters they found. Word of the fighting between monsters and villagers had already reached this village, but the flames of hatred had not been sufficiently stoked here . . . yet.

With pre-arranged lies whispered into ears and the occasional creature sneakily destroyed with NPC weapons, the monsters were soon frothing with hatred.

The sounds of battle now filled the air as the enraged monsters fell upon the villagers, the NPCs doing their best to fight back. Flames licked up the cliff, consuming some of the buildings; many of the fires set by the Broken Eight. The blaze lit the night sky, casting a flickering orange glow on the cliff face, painting flickering shadows across the rocky surface that writhed and squirmed as if the shades were in agony.

Slowly descending, the king of the withers followed his zombie warriors' progress as they ran down the stairs until they reached the ground, then lit the staircase on fire. Flames traveled up the steps, the ravenous maw of the fire devouring everything it tasted.

"Come, my friends, we must continue north, toward the Creeper's Teeth." Krael smiled down at the ancient zombie warriors.

"Why did the king of the withers visit this village?" Ya-Sik asked. "This community could have easily been ignored."

"That's true, but we are starting a revolution." The center head stared down at Ya-Sik while the other wither skulls watched the rest of the zombies. "The discontent we are sowing here will spread throughout this land. Eventually, all the planes of existence in the great pyramid of servers will be in revolt, with monsters taking revenge upon the NPCs for their years of abuse suffered at the villagers' hands." Center smiled at the zombie. "All fires start with a single spark, and that's what we're creating: that spark."

"But why is this necessary? Ya-Sik does not understand."

"When the villagers figure out what we're doing, they'll try to band together, as they did in the Great War." Krael floated closer to the zombie leader, Left and Right watching the monster's sword closely. "But it will be too late. We'll cause chaos everywhere; the NPCs won't be able to come together in their common defense. It'll be pandemonium on every server, and that'll allow us, with the help of my wither army, to move through the servers, destroying every villager, until they are all exterminated."

"But when the wizards—"

Ya-Sik's words were cut off by the moan of a zombie, one the other zombie warriors knew well. Out of the darkness, a gold-clad zombie emerged. His helmet, which was shaped like the head of an enderman, was cracked and dented, as was his shimmering chest plate.

"Ra-Sik, what happened?" the zombie commander demanded. "Where are Pe-Sik and Ne-Sik?"

"Those zombies were destroyed," Ra-Sik said, shaking his head.

"What of the direwolves?" Ya-Sik stepped closer to the zombie, his short sword gripped tightly in his hand.

"All direwolves were destroyed in battle." Ra-Sik lowered his head in shame.

The other zombies gasped in shock, then their surprise was gradually replaced with rage.

"The boy-wizard must have used some trick . . ."

"Maybe used an evil spell . . ."

"Or summoned a demon . . ."

"The wizard and NPCs did none of these things," Ra-Sik said.

"Then how is this possible?" Ya-Sik asked. "The Broken Eight have laid waste to whole villages, destroyed thousands of NPCs, and stopped armies. How is it this small band was able to destroy two of our brothers and three direwolves?"

Ra-Sik took a step backward, away from Ya-Sik.

"The villagers fought like seasoned warriors. They worked together in battle and helped each other, instead of just fighting to save their own lives." Ra-Sik took another step back but bumped into Krael.

The wither glared down at the monster. "Continue, please," Center demanded.

"The wizard had a bow made of bone. That weapon destroyed our direwolves."

"Ahh . . . the bow stolen from the skeleton warlord." Krael nodded in understanding.

"And the wizard had some kind of magical weapon: a spiked ball at the end of a long chain." Ra-Sik reached to his chest plate and ran his hand over the dents and cracks. "That weapon did this to my armor."

Krael nodded, then glanced at the zombie leader. "I know the penalty for failure amongst zombies, but there will be no executions today."

Ya-Sik started to object, but the wither drifted higher in the air, the eyes on each skull glowing bright. This stopped the zombie leader's complaint; he knew this was a prelude to a barrage of flaming skulls.

"We will need every one of the Broken Eight on this mission," Krael said.

"Broken Six," Ya-Sik corrected, then glared at the wounded zombie.

"Yes . . . Broken Six, I suppose." Krael's eyes dimmed as he moved closer to the ground. "Don't worry, Ya-Sik, you'll have your revenge. We'll all have our revenge. I have no doubt the wizard found the map in the Tower of Shadow, and he'll likely know their company cannot climb the Creeper's Teeth. That leaves only one path open to them if they wish to reach the Cave of Slumber before we do."

"And what's that?" a zombie with a helmet in the shape of a ghast asked.

"The Labyrinth." Krael smiled.

"Why would this wizard be foolish enough to enter the Labyrinth?" Ya-Sik asked.

"He's still a boy and knows little about the history of the Great War. And I have seen little written about the Labyrinth in any books; it's possible the truth of the place has been lost to time. Only a full-fledged wizard could hope to survive those passages, and this boy is still very young. He cannot survive."

"Then the wizard and villagers have lost?" Wi-Sik asked, the eyes on his ghast helmet glowing bright with excitement.

"Not yet," Right said. "The wizard may change his mind when he sees the entrance to the Labyrinth."

"That's right," Left added. "The wizard is probably a coward."

"It doesn't matter," Center snapped, taking control of the discussion again. "We are going to make his choice for him. We'll get to the entrance of the Labyrinth before they do, and then we'll ambush them."

Krael stared down at the zombie commander. "All zombies must remove their boots."

"Why?" Ya-Sik replied defiantly, not understanding.

Right scowled while Left hissed something, his eyes beginning to glow as he readied his flaming skulls.

"Both of you be calm." Center glared at the other skulls, keeping their tempers in check, then turned back toward the zombie. "The enchantments used to create you and your armor are extremely powerful. It cost the lives of many zombie warlocks to make these magical items. Their power leaks into everything you touch, including the ground; your boots damage the surface of Minecraft, leaving behind charred footprints. We can't let the boy-wizard know we're waiting for them by leaving a bunch of prints on the ground."

Krael floated closer to the zombie leader and stared into his eyes. "The boots must come off until we reach the Labyrinth. Once we're in position, you and your zombie warriors may put them back on."

Ya-Sik paused for a moment, considering the request, then glanced at the other zombies and nodded. They all removed their golden boots and put them into their inventories.

"Good." The king of the withers smiled. "Now we can sneak past those foolish villagers and spring our trap. The wizard can choose to fight all of us, or flee into those cursed tunnels. I'm sure he will choose the latter and run; he is not foolish enough to try and face all of us with just his puny band of NPCs."

"He will choose the Labyrinth," Right said with a cruel smile.

"They'll never leave those tunnels . . . alive," Left cackled in a scratchy voice.

Center smiled and nodded. "Now, it's time to move . . . fast. All zombies should eat something now, for there will not be time later."

The monsters took out loaves of bread and apples stolen from the villages and ate, quickly devouring the food.

"Everyone, follow me," Krael shouted. "We have a wizard to trap!"

They took off running toward the distant Labyrinth as flames continued to devour the cliffside village above and shouts of pain and fear from the villagers filled the air.

CHAPTER 17

Watcher glanced to the eastern horizon, grateful for the presence of the sun as it rose into the air, even though its harsh light cast pale reds and oranges across the horizon, making the landscape appear stained with colors as bleak as the sun itself. This was not the beautiful spectacle the NPCs were accustomed to seeing at sunrise, but in Minecraft, sunlight was always better than darkness.

They'd run all through the night after leaving the Compass. On the north side of the strange building, they'd come across more of the stone arcs. Half-circles of rock in different sizes dotted the landscape, the strange rings jutting up from the ground like the humps of a gigantic, stone sea serpent. Watcher thought these rocky curves might have been failed experiments by the wizards, but they'd probably never know for sure.

Thankfully, once the sun started to brighten the sky, the intrepid warriors could see trees ahead. None of them enjoyed being near the "stony curves," as Er-Lan called them, and were glad to be entering a forest soon, but as they neared the trees, their feelings of unease grew worse.

"Do all of you see what I see?" Mapper asked.

"Yep." Blaster removed his black leather armor and replaced it with forest green. But when he saw what they were approaching, he replaced it again with dark brown instead.

"It looks like something tore the leaves off all the tree branches," Planter said. "How can that be?"

"I don't know," Watcher said. "Maybe a big storm blew through here and ripped them off."

"Then how do you explain the grass?" Cutter pointed to the ground as they stepped into the forest. "It's all dried up." He reached down and ran his fingers through what should have been green, verdant blades, but were instead gray and brittle. The grass turned to dust with a simple wipe of his hand. "Whatever harmed the trees, it didn't leave out the grass. It's all dead."

"Effects of the Great War, that is what happened here." Er-Lan's voice sounded sad. "I can feel the echoes of terrible pain here."

"You mean there was a battle here, and villagers died?" Cutter asked.

Er-Lan shook his head. "No, what happened here was an attack on the plane of existence itself, and the victim was the fabric of Minecraft. Something tried to damage this forest in hopes of shattering the land. Er-Lan cannot imagine why a wizard would do this."

"A wizard . . . why do you think it was a wizard?" Watcher turned and faced the zombie.

"Er-Lan can tell," the zombie said. "What was done here was by the hands of a wizard, not a warlock."

Watcher started to object, but Er-Lan put a hand on his shoulder. "It is not Watcher's fault, nor is it Er-Lan's," the zombie said. "What happened in the Great War was the fault of our ancestors. Their crimes do not fall upon anyone in this time."

"Well, except for the wither king," Planter said.

"And the Broken Eight," another villager said.

"You mean 'the Broken Six.'" Blaster grinned. "They gotta be renamed now because of us."

"I think we should get through this terrible biome as quickly as we can." Watcher nodded to his friends, then took off running through the dead forest.

The grass under his feet crumbled as he ran, his diamond boots kicking up small clouds of dust. Watcher scanned the forest for signs of life, but only saw the leafless trees and dried, crumbling grass. In places off to the side, he saw areas where the grass was already crushed. The dusty footprints seemed to move parallel to their path; it was likely just cattle or sheep moving through the forest looking for grass to eat.

"I hope we'll be out of this dead forest soon," Planter said. "It gives me the creeps."

"You don't have to be afraid." Fencer smiled at Planter. "I'm sure Watcher will protect us all in case some monster comes out to attack us here."

"I didn't say I was afraid, I said it . . . why am I talking about this with you? Never mind." Planter veered to the right, putting other villagers between her and Fencer.

Er-Lan moved up next to Watcher, the zombie's green feet in lockstep with the boy's.

"I feel the Eight," the monster said.

"You mean the Six?" Watcher said with a smile.

"They will always be the Broken Eight to Er-Lan." He lowered his voice. "They are drawing near."

"You think they're sneaking up on us from behind?"

"Perhaps . . . that was also Er-Lan's thought. A rearguard might be wise, just in case." Fear and uncertainty filled the zombie's eyes.

Watcher motioned for Blaster to come near. "Er-Lan thinks the Broken Eight are getting closer."

Blaster's eyes swiveled from left to right, scanning the dead forest.

"He thinks, and I agree, that a rearguard might be a good idea," Watcher said.

"I'm on it." The boy grabbed two other villagers, then ran back along their trail to check for pursuers and to watch the group's rear, just in case the monsters tried to mount a sneak attack.

"I see something up ahead." Mapper sounded winded, but kept running.

"I see it too," Cutter said. "This dead forest is ending."

Watcher nodded. The leafless trees were thinning out, allowing the next biome to be visible. But instead of another forest, a huge mountain range loomed along the horizon, its tops sheared flat. The mountains were a mixture of grays, with stone, gravel, diorite, andesite, and spots of bedrock mixed in here and there. They all had a completely unnatural look to them, as each mountain butted up against another the same size.

Watcher stopped and stared at the monstrosities.

"Those must be the Creeper's Teeth," Mapper said. "You see all the holes covering the steep faces?"

"Yep." Watcher nodded.

"I bet those are all filled with monsters the likes of which we've never seen." Mapper shuddered and looked away.

"Where's the entrance to this Labyrinth?" Cutter asked.

Mapper pulled out his map. "Watcher, touch the map."

A purple spark leaped from Watcher's finger when he touched the torn piece of paper. Suddenly, the map changed, showing their position and the terrain around them. At the base of one of the mountains, a dark passage was visible on the map. It seemed to burrow under the mountain, then twist and turn as it took a circuitous path beneath the Creeper's Teeth. It crossed over itself so many times, it was impossible to follow; the map would be useless in helping them navigate the maze.

"You sure you can get us through the Labyrinth?" Planter glanced at Watcher.

"Of course he can," Fencer said. "He's a wizard . . . he can do anything."

Planter rolled her eyes again.

"Yeah, I'll figure it out," Watcher said. "After all, what Fencer said is true; I *am* a wizard, and the Labyrinth was made by wizards. It'll be a piece of cake."

Now Cutter rolled his eyes and shook his head doubtfully.

"If the map is correct, the entrance should be right over there." Mapper pointed with a crooked finger toward a large mound of gravel and stone.

Blaster and the others returned from their patrol.

"Nothing behind us. I think the Broken Eight must be somewhere else." Blaster glanced at Er-Lan. "You must have been wrong about feeling them nearby."

"Feelings about the Broken Eight are never wrong," the zombie said in a low, nervous voice.

"Okay . . . let's get moving." Watcher drew Needle, the sparkling weapon instantly feeling as if it were a part of his body. "Follow me."

Leaving the dead forest, Watcher sprinted across the rocky landscape, weaving around large hills of stone and gravel. Some of the mounds were six to eight blocks high, making them difficult to see past. Choosing the easier path, he ran around the hills rather than going over them. As he ran, an uneasy feeling began tingling along his nerves, as if something were trying to warn him. The gauntlets on his wrists, instead of glowing brightly as they had in the forest within the Compass, were now dim, barely giving off any light at all . . . it was strange.

"There's the opening!" Fencer shouted.

Watcher turned and found her at his side again. He looked in the direction she pointed. Sure enough, there was a dark opening between two huge mounds of gravel, their sides steep and impossible to climb. The entrance was jagged and misshapen, giving it the appearance of a large mouth, twisted and warped as if in terrible pain. A wooden sign with dark letters sat above the entrance. Watcher slowly approached it and read aloud.

"Only a *TRUE* wizard can pass through the Labyrinth

unharmed." He glanced at Planter. "What do you think that means?"

"You're the wizard, you tell us." Planter scowled.

Watcher moved a little closer to the entrance, but then stopped and shivered as a strange, chilly sensation crept up his legs, causing little square goosebumps to form on his arms and neck. He stepped a little closer. The opening to the Labyrinth seemed to yawn wider, as if it were trying to devour him, and the chilly feeling spread from his legs to his chest. It was like a thousand little icy spiders were crawling across his skin, pricking him with their frozen, pointed legs.

"I can feel the Labyrinth," Blaster said, his face growing pale with fear. "It wants us to enter, as if it's gonna eat us." He glanced at Watcher. "I don't think I like your little wizard tunnel so much."

"I'm not sure if this is such a great idea either." Watcher's voice was weak and filled with fear.

He turned to his companions. They all had similar expressions on their faces: fear and trepidation.

"Yeah, I think you're right," Planter said, her voice cracking with fright.

A chill spread through the air, making the hairs on the back of Watcher's neck stand up.

"So . . . we meet the boy-wizard again." A screechy voice suddenly filled the air.

Watcher instantly knew who it was: Krael, the king of the withers. He turned with Needle held before him, ready to deflect any flaming skulls, but, with the villagers so tightly packed between the mounds of gravel on either side, a single shot might destroy them all.

"I've been looking forward to meeting with you again." Krael smiled a malicious smile. "That little trick you played in the spiders' lair, shooting an arrow at me with the Bow of Destruction, that wasn't very nice. It's just unfortunate you're a wizard. I would have enjoyed watching the Bow destroy you, as it does all non-wizards."

"I hope that arrow hurt when it hit you," Watcher tried to shout, but his voice was still weak with fear.

"You're a fool," the left skull said in a harsh tone. "Those arrows have a limited range. We just teleported far away, and it eventually just fell to the ground."

"That's right," the right skull added, her voice softer and smoother. "We've been around for a long time, and know much more than you about the artifacts left behind after the Great War. For example, I bet you didn't even know that the famous wizard Dalgaroth made that sword of yours." The skull sneered.

"Of course he didn't know," Left said. "The boy is just a fool pretending to be a wizard."

"Stop your prattling," Center commanded.

"We aren't afraid of you, Krael," Watcher said, his voice regaining its strength as he stepped away from the Labyrinth entrance and moved closer to the king of the withers.

Planter stood next to him, her red shield with the three wither skulls on it in her left hand, ready to deflect any of the wither's flaming skulls, just as she had done in the spiders' lair.

The wither glared at the shield, then smiled. "You think I came alone and that shield will offer any protection? You're all fools." Krael laughed. "Zombies!"

The Broken Eight—though only six were still alive, with just five direwolves at their sides—emerged from behind the mounds of gravel around the group. The zombies snarled at Watcher while the wolves growled, baring their teeth.

Waves of fear crashed down upon Watcher. He remembered what only three of the Eight and three direwolves did to their party, but now there were six of the ancient zombie warriors and the rest of their animals.

I don't know if my wizard powers are strong enough to protect everyone from these monsters, Watcher thought, dread filling his soul. *What do I do?*

The wither king floated higher into the air as the

zombies and direwolves filled in the gaps, eliminating any thought of escape.

"Watcher . . . what's the plan?" Blaster whispered.

The wolves took a step closer, their fur bristling as their eyes glowed bright red with fury.

"Watcher, what should we do?" Blaster's voice was louder this time, sounding scared. "We could really use some of that wizarding power right now."

But Watcher couldn't respond. The zombies and wolves had him terrified beyond thought.

"Ya-Sik, it is time for your fellow zombies and wolves to feed." All three skulls smiled. "Attack!"

CHAPTER 18

Someone grabbed the back of Watcher's armor and yanked him away from the charging zombies, his heels dragging on the ground. Arrows zipped past his head as the villagers fired upon the onrushing wolves. Yelps of pain came from the animals, but they did not slow.

"Hurry, everyone! Into the tunnel!" Cutter shouted.

Watcher pulled the hand from the back of his armor and stood. Shoving his sword back into his inventory, Watcher drew the Flail of Regrets and swung it over his head just as a wolf dived at him, its powerful jaws open wide and its sharp teeth aiming for his throat. Suddenly, Watcher was alive with magical power, the spiked ball at the end of the Flail giving off a bright flash as he swung it into the animal, knocking it across the narrow pass. The wolf flashed red, then tried to stand, but Watcher was already attacking again, bringing the weapon down upon the creature once more. It yelped in pain, then turned and fled.

"Watcher, get in here!" It was Planter's voice . . . she was scared.

Watcher swung the Flail at another direwolf, strik-ing it in the shoulder, then turned and sprinted toward the dark opening. The chilling fingers of dread emanating from the Labyrinth spread across his body again, but he didn't care; getting away from the wolves and zombies was much more important right now.

He dashed across the stony ground and dove into the entrance of the Labyrinth. All the while, archers fired from the opening, shooting at the zombies and wolves. The furry creatures were too fast to hit, dodging the arrows easily. Some of the pointed shafts hit the zombies, but they just pinged harmlessly off their enchanted armor.

"Enjoy your stay in the Labyrinth, fool," Krael bellowed from above.

Just then, the sound of stone grinding against stone filled the passage.

"Look, the entrance is getting smaller!" someone shouted.

Huge blocks of bedrock slowly moved across the opening, one set rising from the ground while another descended from above. The entrance grew narrower and narrower as if the rocky mouth closed upon its prey, until, finally, the entrance disappeared. A thick, oppressive darkness, making them all feel as if they'd lost their eyes, wrapped around the group like a gloomy, impenetrable fog.

Chilling icicles of fear stabbed at Watcher as the darkness seemed to close in around him. He felt completely alone and isolated. Glancing down at his hands, he noticed the iridescent glow of magic that normally pulsed across his arms was now gone. In fact, the Flail of Regrets, still in his hand, was dark as well, its energetic purple radiance now missing. Somehow, the Labyrinth had extinguished all magic, making Watcher feel small and insignificant.

Someone pulled out a torch and held it high over their head; it was Blaster.

"This is nice in here." The boy ran his hands across the rough-hewn stone walls, listening to the sound of water dripping somewhere up ahead. "It could use a little decorating, but so far . . . I really like it."

He smiled, likely trying to lighten everyone's spirits, but it did nothing. Watcher knew everyone in the company felt a chilling sense of dread seeping into their souls. There was something very wrong about these passages, but they had no choice; they were trapped, and now must test their courage against the Labyrinth if they wished to live.

CHAPTER 19

"So what now, wizard?" Blaster asked, the torch in his hand sputtering and sizzling as water dripped from the ceiling and onto the flame.

"I guess we follow the passage." Watcher's voice was timid and uncertain.

"You guess? Is that the best you've got?" Cutter demanded. "You were the one who said this way would be easy. And now we're down here in these tunnels, and you *guess?*"

"Don't be so disrespectful. Watcher will figure a way out of these passages." Fencer tried to get to the boy's side, but with so many villagers choking the passage, it was nearly impossible to move.

"Listen, little girl." Cutter's frustrated voice grew louder, echoing off the tunnel walls. "I was happy to look for a witch and battle the spider warlord and her army to save your life. But I'm not gonna play this game you're playing with Watcher. We're in a difficult situation here, and we need to figure out what to do, and you constantly complimenting Watcher isn't gonna help."

Fencer took a stunned step back, bumping against the wall. She glanced at Watcher, but the wizard said nothing.

"I think it best we see where this passage leads," Mapper said. "Perhaps we should have someone with a torch at the front of the line, one in the middle, and one at the end."

"Now we're talking." Cutter patted Mapper on the back, almost knocking the old villager over. "That's what we need . . . a plan."

Watcher pulled out a torch and worked his way to the front of the group. "I'll lead. After all, it was my idea to come in here; I should be the first to face whatever danger is waiting for us."

No one objected; it made Watcher a little sad. With a sigh, he started walking.

The passage went arrow-straight through the fabric of Minecraft. After traveling maybe twenty blocks, they came to an intersection with tunnels extending out in all four directions. Watcher placed his torch on the wall, marking one of the passages as "explored," but the torch wouldn't stay. It just popped off the wall and landed in his hand again.

"Try placing some dirt on the ground," Mapper suggested.

Watcher tried, but the same thing happened; the block of dirt bounced off the tunnel floor and right back into his inventory.

"So much for marking which passage we've explored and which we haven't," Blaster said, rubbing his chin as he thought. "Maybe I could mark the tunnels with a little TNT. I bet we'd notice a crater if we passed it."

Shaking his head, Watcher glanced at his friend. "We can't do that. The mountain over our heads has a lot of gravel in it. TNT could cause a cave-in, which I'm thinking would be bad."

"Let's just keep moving," Planter said. "We can't be any more lost than we are right now."

There was a stinging tone to her comment, and Watcher knew it was meant for him. He glanced at her, but Planter instantly turned away, choosing to stare at the wall rather than look into his eyes.

With a sigh, he held his torch up high and continued through the tunnel. They came across more intersections as they walked, the other passages looking identical to every other one. Their path remained arrow-straight, the corridor never deviating by a single block. *Maybe it will go on forever*, Watcher thought, but after what felt like hours in the seemingly endless tunnel, the passage finally ended in a large circular room built of obsidian and quartz.

The room felt older than time, as if it had been here since the creation of Minecraft. The air was dank and stale, with dust coating Watcher's tongue with every breath. The chamber itself was at least twenty blocks across, with a complicated pattern of quartz embedded into the obsidian floors and ceiling eight blocks overhead. The walls boasted a zigzag line of quartz around the chamber, the white blocks making the dark surfaces seem less depressing. Bookcases could be found here and there, with numerous dusty tomes on the shelves; clearly, they hadn't been touched for years, if not centuries.

A single block of netherrack, recessed in the floor, burned with perpetual flames, casting a flickering glow throughout the black-and-white room. Iron bars surrounded the fire, keeping the careless from getting burned. Multiple openings lined the perimeter of the chamber, each leading to dark tunnels like the one from which they had just emerged. Tables and chairs lined one side of the room, with wooden chests sitting nearby. On the other side of the chamber, maybe a dozen beds sat on the ground, their red blankets a bright crimson against the dark floor. But the most notable feature in the room was a shining wall of metal standing next to a large bookcase, its surface mirror-smooth.

"Well . . . this is better than the tunnel," Blaster said, looking around. "But it still leaves us pretty much completely lost."

Watcher hung his head down, feeling responsible for their predicament.

"Don't worry; Watcher'll figure it out." Fencer moved to his side, brushing her arm up against his.

Someone giggled, but Watcher didn't look up to see who; he didn't care.

I led my friends into these tunnels thinking I'm some kind of great wizard, he thought. *But now, down here, I'm just like everyone else.* He looked at his arms; the magical power woven into his body was gone . . . maybe forever. *Now, I'm nothing.*

Watcher sighed as tears threatened to burst forth, but he refused to set them free. Choking back his emotions, he raised his head and glanced around the room. All of the villagers were staring at him, waiting for some great plan that would save them all from eventual starvation.

A hand rested on his arm. Glancing down, he found it was Fencer's and stepped away, pulling from her grasp. Watcher turned toward Planter, hoping for something to ease the fear and sadness enveloping his soul, but all he saw was an angry scowl. He looked away.

"Maybe we should try another tunnel?" Mapper suggested. "They must lead somewhere."

"That's a great idea." Cutter pounded his enchanted iron chest plate with his fist. It vibrated like a gong, the echoing sound ringing off the dark walls. "Let's get moving."

Cutter glanced at Watcher, waiting for him to take the lead, but after a few moments of waiting, the big warrior shook his head and chose a passage at random. He charged into the darkness with a torch held over his head, the rest of the NPCs following behind him.

Watcher sighed and got into line, sandwiched between Mapper and Blaster; Planter was somewhere up ahead, and Fencer somewhere behind.

"You need to snap out of it, Watcher." Blaster nudged him in the back. "These villagers need you. We need your courage and creativity. We need your optimism and unwillingness to surrender, and all we're getting from you is defeat."

"Look at my arms." Watcher held his arms out for Blaster to see. "My magic is gone."

"Well, I have news for you," Blaster whispered into his ear. "No one cares about your *magic*. It wasn't your magic that helped defeat the spider warlord. It wasn't some great spell that destroyed the skeleton warlord or Tu-Kar, the zombie warlord . . . it was *you*. Everyone here is counting on *you*, and if you just give up because your arms aren't bright and shiny anymore, then the courage that barely holds our company together will snap. That's when we'll be doomed."

"Blaster is right," Mapper said from ahead of him. "It will start with people arguing with each other; that's how societies always crumble, through internal dissent that cannot be quelled. In these cases, the disagreements will lead to people refusing to talk to one another until, eventually, violence breaks out. This has happened throughout history many times, and it will happen here if we do not have leadership everyone can trust . . . and that's you."

Watcher let the words sink in as he shuffled through the cold and damp passage, the sounds of the group's footsteps bouncing off the stone walls and coming at him from all sides. It was as if he was surrounded and all the echoing voices were pointing fingers of blame at him.

"You don't get it." Watcher took a deep breath and fought for control of his emotions. "I need my magical powers to get us out of here; that's the whole reason why we went into the Labyrinth."

"No . . . I think the huge direwolves and ancient zombie warriors had something to do with that," Mapper corrected.

"And don't forget about the wither," Blaster added.

Mapper nodded. "That's right. Krael was there as well. Did you plan on fighting all of them right there?"

"Well . . . um . . ."

"If we had held our ground, it's likely many of us would be dead." Mapper's voice was growing angry. "We had no choice; the Labyrinth was the only way to keep everyone safe."

"But now look where we are," Watcher moaned.

"That's right, look where we are." Blaster put a hand on Watcher's shoulder. "We're in these terrible tunnels, and none of us have any idea how to get out. But fortunately, we have with us the most clever NPC ever to walk the Far Lands . . . and that's you."

"I don't feel so clever." Watcher lowered his gaze to the ground.

Both Blaster and Mapper sighed as an uneasy quietude came over the company.

"Look, there's light ahead." Cutter's voice shattered the silence. "Come on, let's run."

The villagers sprinted through the rest of the passage, their spirits raising with each step. The tunnel pierced through the bowels of the mountain, heading, as near as Watcher could tell, due east, without ever turning or altering course.

As they ran, Watcher, too, started feeling optimistic. It felt like they were doing something right, that there was an escape at hand and literally light at the end of the tunnel . . . but his hopes began to crumble when he saw where the tunnel led.

The stone corridor deposited them back into another black-and-white circular room, the quartz zigzag pattern running around the circular wall just as before.

Their spirits plummeted.

"Wait a minute," Blaster shouted. "How do we know if this is the same room we had already been in?"

Many of the villagers nodded their heads, seeing his point.

Blaster removed a block of TNT from his inventory and tossed it onto the ground, far from the flames of the central fire. The tiny red and white cube bobbed up and down in place, as if riding on some unseen ocean swells.

"Come on, follow me." Blaster held a torch over his head and dashed into another tunnel.

The rest of the NPCs followed, each of them excited to see what this experiment would yield. They ran in silence, dashing through the corridor like tiny little drops of blood through stone arteries. As before, the tunnel was straight as a beam of light, never wavering to the left or right as it bored through the flesh of Minecraft. After what seemed like hours, a flickering light appeared at the end of the passage.

But, just as before, the tunnel deposited the villagers into another circular black-and-white chamber.

"Look . . . there's Blaster's TNT." One of the villagers spotted the red-and-white striped cube floating off the ground.

Blaster moved to the item and picked it up. He passed it from hand to hand as he glanced around at the other tunnels. Watcher moved to his side.

"What are you thinking?" Watcher asked.

"I'm thinking we're in some trouble here." Blaster pointed at the dark corridors. "I bet if you take any of those tunnels, they'll lead you straight back to here. Kind of an infinite loop."

"Well, wizard," Cutter boomed, "how are we gonna get out of here?"

"Yeah," another soldier said. "How do we escape the labyrinth?"

"Watcher, we need a plan . . ."

"Watcher, think of something . . ."

"Watcher, use your magic . . ."

The NPCs leveled question after question at Watcher, pleading with him to save them. Their voices overlapped with each other until they became a cacophony of words echoing throughout the chamber, and all Watcher could do was stand there and stare at the ground in hopeless despair. Soon, the questions became arguments as villagers debated what to do next. Some wanted to try tunneling out, but Watcher knew that wasn't a viable solution; the wizards who had constructed the Labyrinth would have considered that. Some wanted to send someone through each tunnel at the same time; maybe one of them would escape. But then they couldn't agree which tunnel each person would take.

The arguments became more heated, with shouts turning into pushing, Planter and Cutter separating the angriest of villagers. Planter glared at Watcher multiple times during the chaos, her stares filled with venom. He knew she wanted him to do something, but what could he do? He had no magic, no plan, and no ideas.

Watcher felt as if he were an audience member at some tragic play. He was witnessing his band of comrades fall apart right before his eyes . . . and it was all his fault.

I've failed them all, he thought. *I failed the most important person in the world, Planter. I failed my friends and doomed them to a long, merciless battle with starvation. I'm not a wizard . . . I'm nothing.*

With his hope gone, he moved to the far side of the chamber and sat down in front of the silvery, reflective wall, away from everyone else, and just waited for the inevitability of death to end his misery.

CHAPTER 20

The arguments surged like the weather in the Far Lands, at times a downpour of angry shouts and hurtful insults, but then the disagreements quieted to just a drizzle of hopeless whispers. Watcher felt every comment like daggers to his soul as he sat there. The sense of despair in the room was like a leaden sheet, pushing down on everyone with its relentless, hopeless weight.

"I caused this," Watcher whispered to himself. "This is all my fault."

He slowly raised his head and glanced at the shiny wall before him. He hadn't really noticed it before, but the silvery wall was showing the reflection of the room. A large, dusty sign above the mirror held some menacing-looking words, but he couldn't see it from so far away. Watcher stood and approached the mirror, staring up at the sign. There were only three words, but the thick lettering seemed to scream at him. It said, 'Reflections never lie.'

"'Reflections never lie?'" He was confused.

Moving closer, he looked into the mirror, searching for his likeness. At first, all he could see was the room and the other NPCs behind him. When Blaster's reflection came into view, it didn't look like the Blaster he'd known growing up. Instead, he looked like some kind of legendary warrior, tall, muscular and unafraid of any challenge. At the same time, though, he had a humorous and jovial face, with laughter streaming from his mouth.

And then Cutter moved into view in the mirror. He too resembled some famous, legendary warrior, his arms and chest rippling with muscles. In the reflection, Cutter's armor was completely gone, but in each hand, he held enchanted diamond swords, the blades slightly curved, their razor-sharp edges gleaming, making the need for armor nonexistent. The expression on his face was that of a seasoned fighter daring any enemy to attack and test his skill with the blades.

Just then, Er-Lan moved into the mirror's field of view, and Watcher was stunned by the monster's appearance. An iridescent purple glow enveloped the zombie, the magical radiance pulsing, as if linked to his heartbeat, and a long red cloak with lavish gold stitching zigzagging across it hung down from his shoulders. Under the cape, he wore golden chain mail with blood-red gems attached, creating ornate designs across the chest and arms. It made for a brilliant, glimmering spectacle. Watcher was astounded; the zombie looked like what he imagined one of the great monster warlocks would have resembled.

But then, Watcher noticed himself in the mirror. He too appeared tall and muscular, his towering form looming over the others in the image, with a puffed-up chest and chin held high. Bright stitching of gold and silver decorated his magnificent clothing, with the rarest emeralds and diamonds adorning his shirt and billowing sleeves. Everything about his appearance seemed glorious, except for one thing: he looked hollow inside. His exterior was not supported by anything within; it was just a façade, a fake covering to hide his true self, which lay hidden within the shadow of his empty core.

The reflection turned and stared at Watcher, its eyes as dark as coal. The image pointed at him with a bent finger, as if accusing him of some crime or betrayal. And that's how it felt. The fake-Watcher made the real-Watcher feel as if he'd betrayed all his friends by stranding them here in the Labyrinth.

"Your arrogance did this," fake-Watcher said. "You know you aren't a real wizard; you're just a kid with some magical toys. You're no match for the Labyrinth. And now your self-importance has condemned your friends to a long and terrible death."

The image's voice boomed within his mind, shattering any small confidence or hope still alive within. The words were like a hammer to his fragile, glass soul, cracking it into a million pieces, leaving his raw and vulnerable inner self with all its flaws and weaknesses exposed and staring him in the face.

"No . . . I didn't mean it." Watcher fell to the floor as the terrible image seemed to be growing taller and somehow moving closer. He tried to scoot away, but his legs wouldn't work.

"Watcher . . . what's wrong?" Planter rushed to his side.

When she moved in front of the mirror, her reflection was like a beacon of iridescent purple light. Her long blond hair shimmered like fine gold strands, her emerald green eyes the rarest of gems. Planter's image was complete beauty and perfection; it matched her real self exactly. But when her image turned to look at fake-Watcher, her face took on a pained expression. Fake-Watcher glared at wounded-Planter, then turned away, as if staring at someone else. A voice in the distance told fake-Watcher he was strong and handsome and powerful. It made his image puff up even bigger, while the look of sadness and heartache on wounded-Planter's face almost brought tears to real-Watcher's eyes.

That's what he'd done to her, he realized: he'd injured

the girl he cared for just to get some petty compliments from Fencer.

I'm pathetic, Watcher thought. *I wanted to be important and respected and revered for my magic powers, but instead, I hurt Planter, the most important person in my life, with my selfish need to be something I'm not. How can she ever forgive me? Will she?*

He glanced up at the real Planter. "I never meant any of this to happen," he whispered.

"What are you talking about?" Planter asked.

Watcher pointed at the mirror. She stared at the silvery wall, then turned back to Watcher.

"There's nothing there," she said. "What do you see?"

He turned back to the mirror. Fake-Watcher gazed at wounded-Planter, then began deflating, as if something had punctured his perfect, wizard-like skin. His image shriveled and collapsed, with his arms flailing about in the air as his body grew smaller and smaller. His face contorted, not with pain, but with embarrassment and shame, as he slowly became the same size as everyone else's reflections.

But the collapse continued.

Fake-Watcher continued to shrink, his majestic clothes now too big for his body, hanging off his shoulders like a set of oversized curtains. The jewels embroidered on his shirt fell to the floor and shattered like pieces of old candy: the gems were as fake as everything else. His entire appearance in the silvery wall was a mirage, a disguise to hide his insecurities from his friends, he realized.

For the first time in his life, Watcher had wanted to be important, someone to be looked up to and respected, instead of being the smallest and weakest person in the crowd. He had desired to be the one person everyone turned to in their darkest hour, but he'd failed them all with his pretense of being some great wizard. And now the realization of his true self was a blast of painful reality; he was just plain old Watcher with a bunch of magical toys that no longer worked.

Reaching into his inventory, Watcher pulled out the Flail of Regrets. No voices whispered to him, no magic glow shone out, nothing; it was just a stick with a chain and a spiked ball at the end. Like himself, the weapon was ordinary and forgettable.

He sighed as his image shriveled down to his normal size, until Fake-Watcher looked small and insignificant, just like real-Watcher.

"I did this to everyone," he said, his voice barely a whisper. "I listened to flattery and my ego instead of my friends." He glanced up at Planter. "I should have been talking to the most important person in the world—you—instead of letting all those childlike compliments feed my hungry pride."

"Watcher, it's not your fault," she said. "You just—"

"I just led everyone into the Labyrinth because I thought I was a great wizard, and I'd be able to get everyone out of here." Watcher's voice grew louder. "But the truth is, I'm nothing, and I can't get anyone out."

"Don't say that," a voice said from the other side of the room. Fencer ran across the black-and-white floor and stood next to Watcher. "You can get us out; I know you can. You're the greatest—"

"Fencer, just stop." Watcher held a hand into the air, then climbed wearily to his feet. "I was the cruelest to you. I know you have a crush on me. It's likely because I gave you that Notch apple after you fell, so many months ago. It saved your life, which must have caused you to become attracted to me. I should have stopped it right away, but I didn't, because I liked your constant flattery. But none of that is real, and praising someone just to get their attention is the wrong way to gain friends. You should just be yourself, and I should have been honest with you right away, but I was afraid."

"But Watcher," the young girl protested, "you *are* the greatest wizard in the Far Lands, and I—"

"No more of that." Watcher stared straight into Fencer's eyes. "I don't mean to hurt you, but I'm with Planter, not you. I consider you my friend, but that's all . . . I'm sorry."

"But . . . but I'm . . ."

Watcher shook his head, then turned his back on her. Fencer stood there for a moment, stunned, then ran to the far side of the room and laid down on one of the beds, weeping softly.

With a sigh, Watcher stared into Planter's beautiful green eyes.

"You were right. I should have been honest with her," Watcher said to Planter. "And I should have been honest with you. I liked the compliments, but I know they were hollow and meaningless, just like me. I'm nothing without you."

Planter shook her head, an angry expression still on her face. "You think everything is okay now that you finally told Fencer the truth?"

Watcher didn't understand. This wasn't going the way he thought it would.

"I put up with being embarrassed in front of everyone because you wanted to feel important." She put her hands on her hips, her unibrow furled. "I told you countless times to shut her down, but you didn't listen to me. You made me feel insignificant whenever Fencer was spouting out her compliments, and now you think it will all just be erased because you finally did what you were supposed to do a long time ago?"

"Well . . . um . . ."

"If you think I'm just gonna rewind things and go back to the way it was, you're mistaken. I need to know you're serious about our relationship, and you're serious about me. I won't be taken for granted again."

"Of course not," Watcher said. "I'd never take you for granted . . . not again."

"That's right." Planter took a step closer. "I'm not gonna give you a chance. You need to prove you can be trusted, for me to let you back into my life. I'm not like one of your enchanted wizard things that can be pulled out and used when needed, then just put away in your inventory. I'm a person who has feelings and needs to feel respected too. Until you can prove you're serious about who you are and who you want to be, there is no *us*. There's only you and me, separate."

Watcher let her words wrap around him like a thorny blanket. She was badly hurt; he could see it on her face.

I don't know why I didn't see it before, Watcher thought. *The pain I was causing Planter by ignoring how she was feeling, while at the same time encouraging Fencer, has been there all this time.* He clenched his fists. *I'm an idiot.*

The realization of his stupidity was like a gong resonating within his head. He glanced up at her again, but she just turned and walked off slowly, an expression of pained uncertainty on her square face. With a sigh, he looked at the rest of his friends. Some were still arguing about what to do, while others just sat on beds or chairs, defeated expressions on their faces.

I was a fool with all of them as well. I should have realized my magic abilities are not as important as my own abilities and those of my friends.

He noticed Blaster staring at him. For the first time ever, Watcher saw fear in Blaster's eyes, something he thought he'd never see.

We might have been able to get past this challenge if we'd made a plan and worked together. But instead, I just relied on my magic, which is now gone.

Watcher stared down at his hands, hoping the iridescent glow would return, but they remained dark.

But then something moved above the shiny mirror; a new sign appeared on the wall, with letters not as dark and menacing as the ones before. Moving closer, Watcher read the words: 'Only a *true* wizard can escape the Labyrinth.'

Watcher nodded. He hadn't been truthful with his

friends, and he was going to put an end to that right now.

"Everyone, listen to me." Watcher raised his hands over his head, clapping them together to get their attention. Slowly, the arguments ceased as all eyes turned toward him. "Look, I've been a fool. I let this wizard thing go to my head."

"You think?" Blaster said, the sarcastic smile absent.

Watcher nodded and held up the Flail of Regrets. "I don't know if I really have any magical powers or not, but these ancient relics I have . . . I want to tell you the truth about them." He waited for questions, but instead, an uneasy silence filled the air. "I can hear voices, and they come from this weapon. There is some kind of living mind trapped inside the Flail of Regrets, and it speaks to me."

"What's it saying now?" one of the villagers asked.

"Nothing. All the magic is gone, just like with my sword, Needle, and these gauntlets." He held his arms up for all to see. "I was playing the part of a wizard, but I'm not one. All I have are these magical items and the Flail telling me what to do. I'm a fake. I'm just plain old Watcher, the kid that never fit in anywhere. I just wanted to tell you the truth, so there wouldn't be any secrets between me and all of you."

Blaster pointed to Watcher's hand and opened his mouth to say something.

"Please, Blaster, no more funny remarks. Let me finish." He took a deep breath. "Now, I know this looks hopeless, but we're gonna get out of this Labyrinth somehow." He stared at all his friends, their eyes still filled with hopelessness. "I'm tired of the king of the withers and his terrible zombie warriors destroying everything they touch. It's time they were stopped!"

Blaster drew his curved knives and nodded.

"We're gonna get out of here," Watcher continued, "and we're gonna get to the Cave of Slumber before they do, and then we're gonna teach those monsters that they're messing with the wrong villagers!"

Cutter drew his diamond sword and slammed the hilt against his armor. It banged like a church bell, filling the chamber with sound. The looks of despair began to fade from the NPCs' eyes.

"It doesn't matter if I really have any magic or not, because we don't need magic to defeat our enemies. I don't know why my magic disappeared and I don't care. It was probably—"

"But Watcher, you need to—"

"Please, Blaster . . . let me say what I need to say." Watcher gave Blaster an annoyed glance, then continued. "I'm no one special. I'm just the same as all of you, but I can still fight." He held up the Flail, the spiked ball dangling from the end of the chain. "It's true I have these weapons, and like the Bow of Destruction, only I can use them without being killed, since I am a descendent of a wizard, but that doesn't mean we have to rely on the magic. We're gonna stop those monsters . . . no matter what!"

Cutter banged his sword against his chest again. Some of the other NPCs held their weapons above their heads, ready to take on Krael and his zombies.

"That's great, just *great*, Watcher," Blaster said in a loud voice, "but you need to listen to me now!"

"Fine . . . what is it?"

"Look at your hands."

Watcher held his hands before his face. A soft purple glow wrapped around his fingers, then slowly spread to his palms.

"What does it mean?" Blaster asked.

Watcher shrugged. "I don't know, and I don't care. We aren't gonna just rely on any magic I might have inside me. Instead, we're gonna focus on solving any obstacle we face by using all our skills."

The glow grew brighter, now spreading from his hands to his forearms.

"Look at the Flail." Planter pointed at the weapon in Watcher's hand.

The ancient artifact pulsed with magic power again, casting a purple luminescence around the chamber and giving the black-and-white walls a refreshing, colorful hue.

"This isn't important," Watcher replied. He was about to set the weapon aside when it spoke to him.

The mirror, the Flail whispered. *Speak the truth before the mirror.*

Watcher's eyes grew wide with surprise. Turning, he glanced at the mirror. His image was still there, but now it was the true image of Watcher—not a famous wizard, not a pathetic, deflated villager, but Watcher as he really was.

He moved closer to the mirror and stared at his reflection, then glanced up at the sign on the wall.

"Only a true wizard can escape the Labyrinth," Watcher read.

"What'd you say?" Mapper asked. The old man moved to his side.

"I read the sign up there." Watcher pointed to the letters above the mirror.

"There aren't any signs up there," the old man said. "What are you talking about?"

"You can't see those signs?"

Mapper shook his head.

Speak the truth . . . The words from the Flail echoed in his mind.

Squaring his shoulders, Watcher moved until he was almost nose to nose with his reflection. His nervous breath fogged the mirror, obscuring the image. Taking a deep breath, he spoke in a loud and clear voice.

"I used the magic within me to feed my pride. I used it for fame instead of just helping other people. My over-inflated ego caused me to hurt people I care about and let down my comrades when they needed me most." Someone gasped behind him, but Watcher ignored the sound. "Because of my selfishness and desire for fame and popularity, I trapped my friends in the Labyrinth.

My failure should not sentence them to death; it should only sentence me." More gasps. Someone said something to him, but Watcher didn't hear. A tingling sensation covered his body as if a million little pins were poking his skin. He tried to look past his reflection to see those behind him, but the mirror had fogged up even more, and there was a strange-colored haze across the shiny surface. "I am not a powerful and all-knowing wizard. I'm just me, Watcher, and all I care about now is the safety of my friends. I ask the Labyrinth to save them, and I'll pay the price for my many failures."

He waited for something to happen, but nothing did. Turning, he glanced at Mapper, but the old man had stepped away from the boy, a look of astonishment on his wrinkled face.

"What is it?" Watcher asked. He moved away from the mirror and closer to the old man. "What's wrong?"

"Look in the mirror now!" Mapper pointed at the silver wall.

Watcher turned and gasped, shocked by what he saw.

His hands, arms and chest were aflame with a luminous purple glow. The sparkling field flowed around his upper body as if it were alive, wrapping around his chest, then flowing to his shoulders, then jumping from arm to arm. In his hand, the Flail of Regrets was brighter than a lavender beacon; the light from the spiked ball was nearly blinding.

"What's happening?" Watcher asked.

You spoke the truth, the Flail said. *The Labyrinth heard you. Touch the mirror.*

"What?" he said out loud.

Touch the mirror!

Watcher stepped forward and put his glowing palm on the mirror. Suddenly, the silvery surface disappeared in a blast of bright light. He jumped back, startled, the Flail held ready for combat, but nothing happened. When the harsh light faded, Watcher could see into a new corridor, a set of stone steps leading upward in a sloping passage lit with redstone lanterns.

"Well, look what we have here?" Blaster moved forward and put a hand on Watcher's glowing shoulders. "It seems we needed a wizard—a *true* wizard—after all." Blaster drew his two curved knives and disappeared into the passage.

A huge hand slapped him on the back, almost knocking him over.

"Good goin', Watcher," Cutter said. "I knew you could figure this out. I always had faith in you."

"We all had faith in you." Mapper laid a wrinkled hand on Watcher's glowing shoulder. "I knew you'd realize that what you have inside is more important than any material item. Stuff is just stuff and can always be replaced, but who *you* are, and what *you* can do, is always more important. Just stay true to yourself, and we'll be okay."

Before Watcher could respond, the old man moved into the passage. Planter moved past silently and followed the old man, her body tense.

"Er-Lan knew Watcher would find himself, eventually," the zombie said softly at his side. "This zombie never stopped believing in Watcher, whether there is magic or not."

"Thank you, Er-Lan, that means a lot."

The zombie started walking away, but Watcher placed a hand on his shoulder. "Er-Lan, I saw something strange in that mirror."

The zombie stopped and faced his friend.

"It showed me Blaster's inner self: a courageous warrior, yet also someone funny. It represented Cutter as a proud, legendary soldier who was afraid of nothing."

Er-Lan nodded.

"But it also showed me you." The memory of Er-Lan's image appeared in Watcher's mind. Leaning forward, he lowered his voice. "You looked like a warlock."

"What?"

"You wore a fancy cape and had golden chain mail armor with gemstones attached to it, and you glowed purple, you know, like this." He held up a hand. "What do you think that means?"

"Er-Lan is unsure." The zombie seemed equally puzzled.

"I think it's best if we keep this between us and not tell anyone."

"Isn't the truth a better course?" Er-Lan asked.

Watcher shrugged. "Perhaps, but if the other villagers get the wrong idea, they might become afraid of you."

The zombie nodded. "Yes, Er-Lan understands that. It may be best for now."

"Okay, agreed . . . now, let's get out of here."

Watcher patted his friend on the back, then the two companions strode up the stairs in lockstep, both thankful to be leaving the Labyrinth.

CHAPTER 21

K rael floated away from the Creeper's Teeth, the ancient zombie warriors jumping from block to block behind him as they descended the steep slopes. Many of the Broken Eight had new scratches and cracks in their armor, and a few were limping or holding aching arms. The fighting had been tough, with monsters never before seen in Minecraft inhabiting the caves that peppered the slopes of the blunt mountains.

The sun was crawling up from the eastern horizon, throwing long shadows across the steep sides of the Creeper's Teeth. The sunshine was a relief; climbing the mountains and fighting the monsters in the dark had not been easy on the Broken Eight, but the king of the withers had known the zombies would prevail.

The zombies ran down the final slope with their dire-wolves at their sides, leaving the Teeth behind. Krael could see the sense of relief in their bodies; they had fought through some difficult battles to overcome this obstacle.

The ancient wizards had wanted to stop anyone from ever getting past the Teeth and making it to the Cave of Slumber, so they put every ounce of their magic into creating the most vicious monsters possible to guard the slopes. But the NPC wizards had not planned on the Broken Eight and their wolves assaulting the guards of the mountain. Frequently, the monsters of the Teeth had outnumbered the ancient zombie warriors and wolves, but what the zombies and their animals lacked in numbers they made up for in sheer viciousness and disregard for life. The Eight hacked through the horrific monsters with smiles on their scarred faces, their dire-wolves howling with delight as they tore through count-less opponents while they climbed and then descended the mountains.

"What is this land up ahead?" Ya-Sik asked.

"This, my friend, is called the Wasteland." Krael smiled at the zombie, then floated up into the air. "It's what's left after one of the biggest battles in the Great War. The NPC wizards and monster warlocks battled across these biomes using magic more powerful than anything ever seen before. Their spells laid waste to the landscape, leaving it torn and lifeless."

The zombie leader nodded, looking ahead.

The land was dry and parched, with tiny cracks between the blocks of lifeless soil. Gritty dust blew through the air, the tiny grains biting at exposed skin and stinging just a bit. All around them, the empty husks of dead trees lay strewn upon the ground. Their outer bark remained, but their interiors had rotted away long ago, leaving hollow reminders of the great trees like cemetery gravestones marking their past lives. No green grass or green leaves were visible nearby; everything was pale and dead as far as the eye could see. It was a landscape out of a nightmare, and it stretched as far as the eye could see . . . the wither king loved it!

"There is very little left of the original biomes," Krael said. "Most is warped and distorted, with the life sucked out of the land. In some places, plants might still live, but it is very rare. The Creeper's Teeth were meant not only to keep others from the Cave of Slumber, but also to contain the damage done to the Overworld here."

"It seems the wizards were just as destructive as the warlocks," Tu-Sik said, his creeper-head helmet scratched and dented from the recent battles.

"Perhaps, but not destructive enough, or we wouldn't be here," Right skull said.

The zombie nodded in agreement.

"What is Krael's plan?" Ya-Sik asked.

The zombie moved closer to the ground, but still out of reach of the zombie's sword, just to be cautious. "We'll continue north to the Cave of Slumber. There we will release my army of withers and then destroy the Far Lands and every plane of existence in the pyramid of servers."

"So Krael knows the location of the Cave now?" Ya-Sik asked.

"Well . . . I'll feel its effects when we are near."

The zombie leader scowled.

"Trust me, my friend," Krael said. "The wizards made sure all withers feel the pull of the Cave. It will sense my presence first, then reach out and try to draw me in. Have no fear; we will find the Cave of Slumber."

"What of the boy-wizard?" Ur-Sik asked, the legs on his spider helmet bent from battle damage.

"The boy-wizard will never leave the Labyrinth," Krael said. "He has no idea of its secret, and he's too arrogant ever to figure it out. That wizard and his friends will experience a slow and painful death by starvation; we will never see him again."

"Krael is incorrect," Ya-Sik said, his voice filled with certainty.

"You challenge us?" Left demanded.

The zombie leader ignored the skull and focused his attention on Center. "This zombie felt a magical presence emerge into this world while the Eight were descending the Creeper's Teeth. At first, Ya-Sik thought it was some of the monsters protecting the Creeper's Teeth, but none challenged us with the kind of magical power that was felt." Ya-Sik stared up at Krael. "It must have been the wizard."

"Impossible!" Krael's voice dripped with venomous anger.

"Perhaps . . . but this zombie felt something." Ya-Sik glanced at the direwolves, then back to the wither king and smiled.

"You have an idea?" Krael asked.

Ya-Sik nodded. He glanced at the other zombies. "Ra-Sik, come forward." The zombie with a helmet in the shape of an enderman's head moved to his commander's side. "Ra-Sik battled the wizard and his company at the Compass. Direwolves, gather the scent of our enemy from Ra-Sik."

The direwolves growled, then moved to the zombie. Each sniffed his golden armor, moving from hand to hand and even smelling his shimmering sword and shield. They covered every inch of the zombie's body until one of the animals sniffed the zombie's right forearm and howled. The other animals went to the spot and took in the scent, then howled as well, adding their voices to the majestic, terrifying chorus.

"They found the scent." Ya-Sik smiled, then patted his wolf on the side. "Direwolves, follow that scent until you find the boy-wizard. Destroy everyone in the wizard's company, then destroy the wizard. Leave none alive."

The wolves barked and howled, their voices filled with hungry excitement.

"Attack the wizard and his companions when they are vulnerable. Now go!"

The creatures took off, running across the landscape like furry white missiles tracking a distant target, their padded feet moving noiselessly across the wasteland.

"The wizard will never even hear the wolves coming." Ya-Sik laughed, the other zombies chuckling with excitement.

"Come, then," Krael said. "Let us find the Cave of Slumber. Nothing can stop us now."

The king of the withers floated up into the air and headed for the distant cave, excited thoughts of how he would destroy the Far Lands playing through his evil mind.

CHAPTER 22

Watcher emerged from the passage and stared up into the sky. The pale sun was in the east, having risen while they were exiting the Labyrinth. After the darkness underground, its harsh rays were a shock to their eyes, with many of the villagers having to hold a hand up to block the light until their eyes adjusted. It wasn't clear how many days they'd been underground, but they were definitely glad to be out of those tunnels.

The landscape here was bleak, with the gray blades of grass like skeletons of their former green selves, the hollow trunks of trees sad reminders of their magnificent stature, and the dried-up shrubs like a collection of discarded stickmen, forgotten and useless. When Watcher came out of the tunnel, leaving the Labyrinth behind, he thought the worst was over, but then he beheld the terrible scenery, and it made him and all of his comrades sad.

"What happened here?" Planter reached down and tried to scoop up a handful of grass, but the normally soft and pliant blades just crumbled to dust, staining her fingers with an ashen smear.

"I'm not sure," Mapper said. "Maybe some kind of disease that attacked the plants or—"

"Look at the soil." Blaster brushed aside the crumbling grass to reveal the dirt underneath. Instead of the block being a speckled combination of different brown and tan hues, it was a lifeless gray upon gray.

"Even the soil was damaged." Mapper shook his head sadly, then glanced at Watcher. "Any ideas?"

Before Watcher could speak, Er-Lan stepped forward.

"There was a great battle between the wizards and the warlocks," the zombie said. "Er-Lan can still feel the echoes of power that clashed together here." The zombie put his hand on the ground, then closed his eyes, and his face contorted as if in pain. When he opened them, a lone tear tumbled down his scarred face.

"Watcher . . . put a hand on the ground and listen." The zombie moved to his friend's side, then grabbed his hand and pressed it to the dusty surface. Others followed Er-Lan's lead, Planter included, each pressing a hand to the ground and closing their eyes.

Watcher wiped away a patch of grass and pressed his palm to the lifeless ground, then closed his eyes and listened. At first, all he heard was the beat of his heart and his raspy breath going in . . . and out . . . and in . . . and—

Then he heard it.

There were screams of terror followed by great blasts of power, like a million suns torching the surface of Minecraft. The searing heat and blistering winds and great balls of lightning all tore mercilessly into the ground as the NPC wizards battled with the monster warlocks. Watcher could feel the hopeless fears of the wizards in their magical attacks, but there was also terrified desperation in the monsters' responses, as if this was their last chance for survival. Sorrow and despair rained across the land like a plague, crushing the hopes of all whom the battle touched. Something terrible had indeed happened here, but not just in this place; it had encompassed much of this world.

Watcher wiped away a tear as he stood, the terrified emotions he'd sensed almost too much to bear. He glanced at the villagers to see if any of them had felt the same thing, but they only looked unconcerned, except for Planter. She too had a tear in her eyes, but she quickly wiped it off her cheek as she turned away.

"I felt it," Watcher said to the zombie in a sad voice.

"Er-Lan is sorry. It was hoped only Er-Lan could feel the destruction in that battle, but it seems Watcher's powers allow for this." The zombie placed a gentle hand on Watcher's shoulder, consoling his friend.

"I think we need to get moving." Watcher turned to Mapper, anxious to leave this place behind. "Does the map show the location of the Cave of Slumber?"

The old man pulled out the map, then moved next to the boy.

"Touch it while you're thinking about our destination." Mapper extended the map toward Watcher.

He reached out and placed his hand on the map while closing his eyes and focusing his thoughts on the Cave. Watcher had no idea what it looked like, but, somehow, a strong image of it came into his mind. It was a spherical cave, with hundreds upon hundreds of withers floating in the air, each motionless and apparently asleep. It looked as if they had all been flying in the same direction when they fell asleep, as if the horde of monsters had been trying to get to something bright and golden sitting on a ledge at the far side of the chamber.

"You did it," Mapper said.

The old man pulled the map away as Watcher opened his eyes.

"Look . . . there it is, to the north and a little to the west." Mapper pointed with a wrinkled finger.

Watcher glanced over the old man's shoulder. "What are those dots between the Cave and us?"

Mapper shrugged. "Who knows. It's probably just the landscape." He tucked the map away. "We need to go that way." He pointed with a crooked finger to the northwest.

"Okay, let's get moving." Watcher reached into his inventory and pulled out the Flail of Regrets, just to be safe.

They moved in silence through the dead landscape, their boots kicking up tiny clouds of soot around their ankles as their feet crushed the grass to dust. The airborne powder was gritty and coated the back of Watcher's mouth as he breathed. He coughed, as many others did, trying to clear their throats, but it did little good. Reaching into his inventory, Watcher pulled out a flask of water and took a gulp. The liquid washed away the grime, only for it to be replaced with his very next breath. Frustrated, he put the bottle back into his inventory and continued to walk, trying to ignore the foul taste in his mouth.

They walked in silence through the gray landscape as the sun slowly crept higher into the sky. By noon, they'd come to the end of the ashen grasslands and entered a new biome. It was a desert, with the occasional rolling dune interspersed with long stretches of hard-packed sand and sandstone. Watcher almost felt grateful to be leaving the dead grasslands until he stepped into the new landscape and felt the full might of the desert sun.

The blasting heat made many of them stagger as sweat instantly poured down their foreheads. Occasional errant beads of moisture managed to seep their way past their thick unibrows and flow into their eyes, stinging terribly. More than one NPC tried to wipe the painful sweat from their eyes with their sleeves, but with their garments soaked with perspiration, it did little good.

"Watcher, did you notice the ground?" Blaster asked.

Watcher glanced down as he walked. The sand was a pale, off-white color, with different shades of white, beige and pale yellow making up the cube. "It looks normal enough to me."

"Tap it with the heel of your boot."

Watcher stopped his march and tapped the sand with his diamond boot, expecting his heel to dig into the sand, but instead, the cube rang out, as if it were a block of iron.

"What?" He knelt and ran his hand across the hot surface. "It's glass."

Blaster nodded. "Whatever happened here, it melted the top layer of sand into glass."

The other NPCs kicked the ground and knocked on the sand with gloved fists, but no grains came loose; everything was fused solid.

"Strange that so much damage happened on this side of the Creeper's Teeth," Mapper said. "I don't remember seeing any harm like this on the southern side."

"Maybe there were two purposes for the Creeper's Teeth," Planter said. "Maybe they not only served as a barrier to keep people away from the Cave of Slumber, but also as a way of containing the damage from the Great War."

"That's a great theory," Mapper said, nodding.

Planter smiled.

"Thanks," she replied. "I was just thinking that—"

"Er-Lan smells something," the zombie interrupted, sounding alarmed. "It is not right."

"What is it?" Watcher moved to the zombie's side. He glanced at Planter and gave her a grin, but she looked away.

"Er-Lan has a strange memory of this aroma from long ago." The zombie sounded troubled.

"You mean from when you lived in your zombie town?" Planter asked.

He shook his head. "No, the memory is from long, long ago, somehow . . ."

Just then, a moan floated over the next dune, followed by the clicking of a spider and the rattling of bones.

Watcher crouched as he drew the Flail of Regrets, then approached the dune. Laying uncomfortably on the hot, glassy surface, he crawled to the top of the mound and peered over the top.

Below, something akin to a fountain spewed sparkling particles into the air. Beneath the shimmering spray, a collection of monsters bathed in the spray, a look of contentment on each face. But it wasn't just a bunch of zombies, spiders, and skeletons; instead, this group of monsters was a mish-mash of different body parts: the head of a zombie on a spider, a shadowy enderman head atop a skeleton body, a zombie with skeleton arms . . . It was as if the monsters had been disassembled and then put back together in the most random way.

The horrific creatures glanced at Watcher and his friends but didn't take even the smallest step toward them. They seemed to be blissfully content within the twinkling shower, either unwilling or unable to move.

Watcher slowly stood, still expecting the jumbled creatures to attack, but they remained motionless. The other villagers moved to the top of the dune and stood at Watcher's side, all with weapons drawn, but again, the monsters remained within their glittering shower.

"I guess they aren't gonna attack," Blaster said. "Let's just walk around them."

They headed down the dune, but as soon as they'd walked three steps, the shower of sparks suddenly stopped. The monsters glanced around at each other, uncertain, then turned and focused their disjointed and mismatched eyes on the intruders.

"The HP fountain stopped because of them," a zombie head growled from atop a skeleton body. "It will not turn back on until we destroy the intruders."

The other monsters growled and snarled as they slowly stepped away from the now-silent shower.

"We don't want any violence," Watcher said. "We're just passing through. After we leave the area, I'm sure your HP fountain will turn on again."

The mob took another step forward, their eyes filled with a hunger for violence.

"I think they don't believe you so much," Blaster said.

"Yeah . . . I get that impression." Watcher stepped forward and raised the Flail of Regrets over his head, waiting for the monsters to fall upon them, the bitter taste of battle on his lips, again.

CHAPTER 23

Watcher charged forward, the Flail glowing bright purple as he swung it. The spiked ball smashed into the front line of monsters, making them flash red with damage. A fire arrow zipped over his shoulder and struck a zombie, then another flaming shaft followed, taking the last of the creature's HP. It disappeared with a look of confusion on its face. Glancing behind, he found Planter standing there with another arrow already notched.

Beside Watcher, Cutter tore into the monsters with his diamond sword, cleaving into one creature after the next, while Blaster dashed between the monsters, striking out at the creatures with his curved blades. The terrifying monsters tried to stop him, but Blaster was just too fast.

The rest of the warriors formed a battle line, refusing to yield as the horde crashed upon them like a tidal wave of claws and fangs. Villagers shouted out in pain and were pulled out of the line only to be replaced by others. Mapper and Fencer stayed at the rear, helping the injured by offering food and healing potions.

"Everyone . . . move forward!" Watcher shouted. "Advance!"

Slowly, the line of NPCs moved down the dune, pushing the monsters back. When they reached the bottom of the dune, Watcher pulled out his bow.

"Everyone . . . retreat back up the hill!"

The villagers obeyed, turning and running back up the hill. The monsters, not expecting this, just stood there for a moment.

"Now . . . use your bows!" Watcher fired three quick shots at a skeleton. The monster disappeared before it could return fire.

The villagers pulled out their bows and fired down upon the nightmarish creatures as they trudged up the hill in pursuit again. Their pointed shafts chiseled away at the monsters' HP, causing more to fall and disappear. The archers were wreaking terrible damage on the attackers, yet the monsters never slowed, as if the risk of destruction was insignificant compared to their need to get their fountain turned on again. They continued to advance under the hail of arrows until only one creature remained. It was a creature with a skeleton body, dark enderman arms coming off each shoulder, and a spider's head sitting atop its bony shoulders.

Watcher held up a hand, stopping the attack, then stepped forward.

"You need not continue to fight." He lowered his bow and advanced. "We have won the battle, and will now be on our way."

The monster stared at Watcher with its eight blazing red eyes. It unclenched its dark fists, then glanced over its shoulder at the silent HP fountain.

Watcher moved closer. "We'll be on our way. Just step aside, please."

The creature brought all eight spider eyes to bear on Watcher, then clenched its enderman fists and sprang forward.

A flaming arrow streaked past Watcher's ear and struck the monster in the chest. Another arrow flew past, the magical flames singeing his hair, and struck the monster in the shoulder, making it flash red one last time, then disappeared, a look of relief on the monster's terrifying face.

"Nice shooting, Planter," Blaster said as he put away his bow.

"Yeah . . . that was awesome," Fencer added in awe.

Planter glared at the girl, then her face softened, and she nodded.

Watcher moved to her side. "Thanks! You have incredible aim. Those arrows just barely missed me. I'm glad you hit what you aim at."

Planter smiled. "Maybe I missed."

Watcher stood silent, unsure how best to react. But then Planter laughed aloud. Blaster patted her on the back and laughed too, pointing at Watcher's confused face.

"You should see the look on your face," Blaster said. He reached out and punched Watcher in the shoulder. "Come on, let's get moving."

Suddenly, a sound like tiny gems being dropped on the ground filled the air as the HP fountain began working again. Little shimmering sparks shot up out of a hole in a pale block. They flew high into the air, making graceful arcs until they fell back onto the hard ground. Er-Lan moved closer to the fountain and extended an arm with a single outstretched finger. One of the glistening sparks landed on his finger, then soaked into his skin. A smile spread across his face as the HP regenerated his health.

Mapper moved to his side and glanced at the satisfied expression on his scarred face, then stuck a finger out as well. A single shard of HP landed on his finger, and, just like with Er-Lan, Mapper smiled as it soaked into his body.

"You all need to come try this," Mapper said to the rest of the group.

The old man and the zombie slowly moved farther into the HP shower with arms outstretched. Cutter moved to the edge of the shimmering spray and held out a hand. As with the others, a serene smile grew across his square face as the sparks of HP sank into his skin. He too stepped into the fountain, allowing the spray to envelop him.

The other villagers came forward and walked into the spray too, each enraptured by the effects of the HP fountain.

"I think we should get moving," Watcher said, still outside of the fountain's range. "Mapper, Blaster . . . let's get moving."

The two villagers didn't move and made no attempt to answer. Their eyes were glassed over, mouths hanging agape as they just absorbed the HP in what appeared to be sheer ecstasy.

"Come on . . . Planter, Fencer . . . we need to get moving," Watcher said, starting to grow concerned.

Neither of the girls moved. They just stood there, either unable or unwilling to respond.

"It's like a drug," Watcher whispered to himself.

They are in grave danger, an ancient voice said in the back of his mind.

Watcher glanced down at the Flail. *What do I do?* he thought.

Cover the fountain, the enchanted weapon said.

Cover it . . . how? But the Flail remained silent.

"How can I cover it? If I step into the fountain, it'll probably paralyze me, just like all the others."

Watcher searched his inventory for something that might help or maybe trigger an idea, and his fingers brushed against the Elytra wings his sister had given him before they left their village. This gave the young wizard an idea.

Pulling out the wings, he stared down at the shimmering item. He could still hear her words in his mind from the day she gave the fragile wings to him: "Use them when walking just won't do."

"That's exactly the situation now, sis," Watcher said to no one.

He removed his diamond chest plate and strapped the wings to his back, then ran back to the top of the sand dune and planned his attack. Putting away the Flail, Watcher pulled out a block of dirt.

"I'll probably get only one shot at this."

Holding the cube firmly in his hands, he ran across the dune, then jumped up into the air. Leaning forward, he made the wings snap open. As soon as they caught the wind, he started to rise, the breeze rushing past his ears. He banked to the left, then lined up on the gap between Blaster and Cutter. Leaning forward, he traded altitude for speed, though he didn't have much of the former. The wind's speed increased, sounding like a mini-hurricane as it whooshed past his ears.

Gritting his teeth, he entered the HP fountain. Suddenly, the sound of the wind died away, and all he could hear was the tinkling of HP shards dancing across the ground. His skin tingled as the sparkling crystals of health instantly rejuvenated him; it was spectacular.

I could just stand under this fountain forever, Watcher thought. *In fact, I think I'm gonna—*

Drop the block now, the Flail said in his mind. *PLACE IT ON THE FOUNTAIN!*

The enchanted weapon's voice was that of an enraged giant. It shocked Watcher back into his mind again.

Waiting for just the right instant, he placed the block of dirt onto the fountain's mouth as he flew over. Then, out of control, he smashed into the ground in a wash of sparkling particles, flashing red and taking damage, but the sparks of HP still in the air fell upon him, quickly repairing the damage.

Watcher smiled and stood as the bright splashes of light danced upon his body for a moment more, but then the shower ceased; the block of dirt sat right on top of the fountain, blocking its flow. As his mind's clarity returned, he shook his head, trying to clear the numbness from his brain.

"The fountain . . . we need to get away from the fountain."

Watcher reached out to the nearest villager; it was Planter. He grabbed her by the shoulders and shook her. Her eyes blinked, and then the blank expression on her beautiful face faded away.

"What happened?" she asked.

"The HP fountain—it captured everyone," Watcher said. "We need to get everyone away from it before it starts up again." He glanced down at the block of dirt. Tiny cracks were already forming across its brown face. "Shake 'em to wake them up, fast!"

He moved to another NPC and shook them violently. Planter saw what he was doing and copied the action. In seconds, four of them were awake, then eight, then all of them. The group rushed away from the fountain just as the block of dirt shattered and the shimmering sparks shot up into the air again.

"What happened?" Mapper's voice sounded groggy and tired.

"The HP fountain captured all of you. I covered it with a block of dirt, then Planter and I woke you up." Watcher removed the Elytra and put them back into his inventory, then put his diamond chest plate back on.

"I don't think we would have ever left that fountain," Fencer said, shaking her head.

"That's why the monsters fought so hard," Blaster said. "They didn't care if they died or not; they just wanted the fountain back on."

"Why would this thing be here?" Cutter asked.

"Er-Lan thinks it is another of the wizards' defenses," the zombie said. "Attackers either are defeated by the prisoners of the HP fountains, or become ensnared by its power."

Watcher nodded. "We need to be more careful and keep our distance next time. Now let's get moving. We have a Cave of Slumber to find and a certain wither to destroy."

Blaster smiled and patted him on the back, then took off running, the rest of the company following. None of them noticed the beady red eyes loping along, watching them from a distance, each pair filled with a hunger for violence.

CHAPTER 24

They continued northward, consulting the torn map occasionally to make sure they were on course. The entrance to the Cave of Slumber was getting closer and closer; soon they would be there, which made Watcher nervous.

What kind of trap will Krael have set for us when we've reached our goal? Watcher thought. Shivers of fear ran up and down his spine. He shuddered ever so slightly, then glanced around to see if anyone saw.

There was no doubt it would eventually come to a showdown between him and Krael. The Broken Eight and their direwolves were a problem, but they'd already proven they could be destroyed, whereas the king of the withers . . . that was another matter. Somehow, Watcher had to figure out how to destroy Krael if he was going to protect his friends.

The hardened, glassy desert gave way after a time to a lightly forested grassy plain. Rolling hills of green spread out before them, with a random scattering of birch and oak trees, each standing tall and proud. After being in the gray, dead forest, and then the melted desert, this biome seemed like perfection. Some of the NPCs trimmed the leaves on the oak trees, looking for apples, but they found only a few.

As they ran, Watcher noticed a change in the surroundings. The colors of the trees and grass began to fade, although not like the dead forest. Instead, the landscape became grayer and grayer until everything seemed petrified.

"Look at this." Blaster tapped on the leaves of a tree with one of his knives. It sounded as if he were tapping on a block of iron. "It's all stone."

"Even the grass is petrified," Cutter said. The stocky warrior kicked at a clump of tall grass. His iron boot bounced off the blades, not even leaving a dent, but he did it again and again until the grass shattered into a million little granite shards.

"What could cause something like this to happen?" Mapper asked.

"This is likely from the Great War again." Planter's voice sounded angry. "I don't like what this magic has done to the land. All this mindless destruction from a bunch of power-hungry wizards and warlocks makes me sick. Maybe it's a good thing all the warlocks and wizards from the Great War are gone." She glanced at Watcher. "No offense."

He just shrugged. He understood how she felt.

They moved in silence through the petrified forest, an uneasy tension spreading over the group. Everything was so bleak and lifeless; it left a depressing wound in Watcher's soul that seemed to grow larger with every step. Glancing at the other villagers, it was evident by the expressions on their faces that they were feeling the same thing. But, thankfully, after they'd been walking for an hour, the color slowly faded back into the landscape until everything was green and alive again, as were their spirits.

"I can't imagine what kind of spell could have done that stone-making thing to the landscape," Cutter said.

"The more interesting question would be, why did they do it?" Mapper said.

Watcher nodded his head but said nothing. He could still feel the anger in Planter over both his behavior with Fencer and the damage to the landscape. Somehow, he had to make it right.

"Hi," Watcher said as he moved to her side. "That was pretty terrible back there."

She just grunted a response.

The forest around them was getting denser, with the birch and oaks getting closer together.

"You know, I feel terrible about how I treated you." He tried to look her in the eyes, but Planter just stared straight ahead. "I was wrong in listening to Fencer and not shutting her down. You were right to be upset, and I'm going to make it up to you."

"How . . . how are you going to make it up to me?" Planter eyes were filled with anger, but also emotional pain.

"Well . . . I'm just gonna be truthful all the time," Watcher said. He steered around a tree, with Planter going around the opposite side. "I can't change what I did, but I can change what I'm gonna do, and that's treat you with the respect you deserve."

"What about all this wizard stuff?" she asked.

"Well . . . I know I'm not some great wizard, but I do have powers . . . I know it."

Watcher reached out and took her hand in his. She stared down at their intertwined fingers for a lingering moment, then pulled away.

"I *am* a wizard; I just have to understand my powers. Then I can do some good with my abilities."

"I'm not a fan of magic, especially after what we just saw." Planter pointed back at the petrified forest. "The land was lifeless . . . that's a result of magic. I don't see any good coming from a power that can do that."

Watcher started to object, then stopped and considered his words. "Maybe you're right. But if I don't understand my powers, then I can't avoid doing something like that."

"Well, I guess understanding your powers, if you really have any, could be—"

A growl floated through the air, coming from up ahead, causing everyone to stop in their tracks and glance around at the surrounding forest. The trees had grown close together, making it difficult to see things far away.

Another growl came through the woods, but this time from behind. Watcher turned and faced the rear of their formation as Planter stared toward the front. Both pulled their enchanted weapons from their inventories, Watcher holding the Flail of Regrets while Planter gripped her enchanted bow firmly.

"Can anyone see anything?" Watcher whispered.

No one spoke.

"It is the direwolves . . . Er-Lan can feel them," the zombie moaned.

Another growl crept out of the woods and floated past their ears. This one came from the left and was followed by a snarl to the right.

"They're all around us," one of the soldiers said, voice full of fear.

"Stay together," Watcher said. "We can't let them divide us."

Another growl filtered across the forest, flowing on the persistent east-to-west wind.

"There's too many of them," the soldier said. "We have to run!"

"Hold your position!" Cutter boomed.

But the villager didn't listen; he just ran off into the woods, fleeing the last growl he heard. "Everybody run, they're all around us!"

The crunch of the NPC's feet on the leaf-covered ground was easy to hear as he sprinted, weaving around the close-packed trees. But then another crunching sound came to Watcher's ears. It was softer, as if something was gliding lightly across the forest floor. Then more of the soft sounds added to the first as angry growls drifted across the forest, followed by a terrified shout.

"There's five of them, and they're—"

Suddenly, the villager screamed, then went silent. Even the crunching of leaves stopped; the forest grew completely silent . . . like a graveyard.

But then, a victorious howl cut through the silence like a razor-sharp knife through flesh.

"Everyone, move close together," Watcher whispered. "The direwolves want us to run, so they can pick us off one at a time . . . but we aren't gonna do that, are we?"

No one answered, but Watcher knew they understood.

The NPCs formed a tight circle with Mapper and Fencer in the middle, each holding potions of healing at the ready.

The growls moved closer, then spread out in a circle around them. A red blush spread across the sky as the sun kissed the western horizon. Normally, it would have been a beautiful sight, even here, but with the terrifying direwolves slowly surrounding them, the crimson sky reminded Watcher too much of blood. His nerves felt electrified with fear as his pulse quickened. Breathing in short, nervous gasps, he glanced over his shoulder, searching for Planter. He found her sandwiched between Blaster and Cutter.

Good; she'll be safe there, I hope, he thought.

Just then, wolves slowly emerged from the darkening forest, their beady red eyes glowing bright with hatred and a hunger for XP.

"Fight together and watch each other's backs." Watcher's voice cracked with fear, but he knew the other NPCs were feeling the same thing.

Pulling a shield from his inventory, Watcher held it in his left hand, the Flail gripped firmly in his right.

The wolves glared at him with such vile hatred, it was almost painful to look back. It reminded Watcher of the way the bullies used to stare at him when they were getting up the courage to torment him. He swore he'd never forget how those thugs in their village had made him feel, and these wolves were doing the same. Rage bubbled up from within his soul, pushing the fear aside.

"I'm tired of being afraid of these flea-ridden dogs," Watcher said from between gritted teeth. "It's time we taught them a lesson about respect."

The other villagers cheered, some of them banging their swords against their chest plates.

"Come on, you filthy wolves!" Watcher shouted. "Time for you to get schooled."

The largest of the wolves growled, its sharp teeth bared, then let out a piercing howl. At that moment, the direwolves attacked.

CHAPTER 25

The wolves charged at the villagers with jaws snapping and teeth gleaming. Some villagers tried to shoot at them with arrows, but the animals juked left and right, avoiding the pointed shafts. Watcher spun the Flail of Regrets over his head, hoping for advice from the mystical entity living within the weapon, but the ancient voice was silent.

A wolf snapped at the villager next to him, the animal's sharp teeth clamping down on the NPC's sword arm. Watcher smashed the animal with his Flail, hitting it with a glancing blow and pushing it back. The direwolf growled and faced Watcher, then lunged. Rolling to the side, Watcher stood and slammed the spiked ball down, but the animal was expecting that and was already gone.

Suddenly, pain surged up Watcher's leg as a set of powerful jaws grabbed hold of his calf. The animal was too close to use the Flail, so he dropped it and pulled Needle from his inventory, then slashed at the monster, causing the wolf to flash red as it yelped in pain. The creature released its painful grip and backed away.

Shouts of pain came from the other villagers around him as the wolves darted in and out of their formation, snapping at arms and legs with vicious accuracy. The NPCs tried to keep them back, but the wolves were too fast. Though there were only five of them, it seemed like a thousand in the heat of battle. The animals darted across the battlefield like furry white shafts of pain, their teeth slashing at villagers as they passed. But the largest of the direwolves seemed focused solely on Watcher.

The huge beast leaped forward, trying to tear Watcher's sword from his grip; he brought his shield up just in time to deflect the animal's attack. The bands of metal across the shield groaned and cracks formed across the back as they repelled the animal's bulk.

More shouts of pain and fear came from his companions. The sound of healing potions shattering against the backs of his friends filled the air; Mapper and Fencer were trying to help where they could. But the painful yells from his friends were still growing stronger. The wolves were doing a lot of damage . . . he had to do something.

Use the Gauntlets, a voice said in his head.

The direwolf pack leader lunged at him again. He brought the shield up, letting the animal crash into it. The wooden rectangle shattered into a million pieces, the splinters stinging his face. Landing on his chest, the direwolf's paws pressed into his stomach, its hot breath panting in his face. But then a flash of green streaked by, knocking the big animal to the ground. Watcher quickly stood, only to find Er-Lan wrestling with the creature. The wolf snapped at the zombie, but Er-Lan was too quick, narrowly avoiding its sharp teeth. Pushing the wolf away, Er-Lan ran to another villager's aid, his claws, curiously, not extended . . . strange.

Watcher slashed at the huge wolf with Needle, but somehow, the animal caught the blade in its teeth and tore it from his grasp. The monster tossed the blade aside, then snarled at Watcher, an expression of excitement on its lupine face.

Use the Gauntlets of Life, the voice said again, though this time it sounded farther away.

Watcher glanced at Needle on the ground and knew it was the source of the voice: another mind trapped within an enchanted weapon.

The direwolf took another step closer, its hind legs tensed, ready to pounce on him. Glancing down at the gauntlets on his wrists, Watcher held up his hands and pointed them at the monster. Pouring all of his thoughts and his powers and his soul into the gauntlets, he imagined them spitting fire at the wolf. Suddenly, the Gauntlets of Life burst into life, giving off a bright flash that blinded the wolf for a moment. Before it could move, a shaft of purple lightning sprang from the gauntlets and struck the monster, knocking it to the ground.

Watcher gritted his teeth, ready for the pain to come; he knew the more powerful ancient weapons used the wielder's HP as a source of energy, and when the relics drank in that energy, it hurt. But this time, instead of being enveloped in agony like whenever he used the Fossil Bow of Destruction, he found the ground under his feet was growing colder instead.

The direwolf stood again, baring its teeth and growling. Watcher fired another bolt of iridescent lightning, hitting the animal with pinpoint accuracy. The creature flashed red again, but refused to flee; it just came forward, a snarl on its enraged face. Firing another bolt of magical energy at the creature, Watcher advanced, the ground growing colder and harder under his feet.

The purple lightning struck the direwolf hard, knocking it backward. The creature howled in pain and frustration, then leaped toward Watcher, its jaws open and its razor-sharp teeth aimed at his throat.

Gathering all his strength, Watcher threw as much power as he could at the creature. A bolt of purple electricity streaked through the air and hit the wolf, making it flash red over and over until it just disappeared in midair, leaving glowing balls of XP falling to the ground.

Watcher glanced around at his companions. The four remaining wolves were still attacking, with piles of items on the ground around them where NPCs had perished. He moved toward the wolf nearest Planter and attacked with the Gauntlets of Life. Purple lightning stabbed at the vicious creature, making it yelp in pain. The direwolf turned toward its attacker, but never got a chance to move; Cutter swung his diamond sword at the creature while Watcher sent another burst of power at the animal, destroying it. The ground grew cold as the Gauntlets of Life drew energy from the very fabric of Minecraft.

Planter glanced at Watcher, a look of surprise on her face, and started to say something, but he didn't hear. Running toward the next wolf, Watcher sent more bolts of magical power at the creature, striking the animal in the side and knocking it to the ground. As it struggled to its feet, the villagers fell on it, iron swords tearing into the animal's HP. It flashed red over and over, then turned and fled. The remaining two wolves growled, but they also fled as Watcher chased after them, throwing balls of purple energy at them.

"Watcher!" Planter's voice sounded scared.

Instantly, he stopped the pursuit and returned to his friends. When he reached the villagers, he found them circled around two piles of discarded weapons and tools floating up and down just off the ground. Watcher moved next to Blaster and stared at the items.

"Who was it?" he asked.

"Fletcher and Cobbler," Blaster replied.

Watcher slowly raised his hand into the air, fingers spread wide, as his friends did the same.

"They died trying to keep the Far Lands safe from Krael and his monsters," Mapper said.

The other NPCs nodded in remembrance.

No! They died because I couldn't protect them, Watcher thought. *I have these powers, but I don't understand how to use them.* Feelings of frustration mixed with grief filled his soul.

Mapper retrieved the items and distributed the food and weapons amongst the survivors while Watcher walked to where the Flail of Regrets had fallen and picked it up. Putting it back into his inventory, he retrieved Needle, too. Staring down at the blade, Watcher could now sense a presence inside it. It was as if someone or something was living within the sword.

"Watcher, you want to explain what happened over here?" Planter's voice sounded angry.

Looking up, Watcher spotted her and moved to her side.

"You mean destroying the wolves?" Watcher said. "Well, I used the Gauntlets of—"

"Not the wolves . . . look." Planter's voice had an accusatory tone. She pointed at the ground. "That's where you were standing when you blasted the wolf that was attacking me. Now look at the ground."

Watcher glanced down and found a wide gray area that had once been healthy green grass . . . but now was petrified into stone. The tree that stood nearby was also a dreary gray, its once-vibrant green leaves now turned, like the grass, into stone.

Watcher crouched and ran his hand across the cold, hard ground. It was all turned to stone, as if something sucked the very life from the soil, just like in the petrified forest.

"There's another circle of stone over here," Blaster said.

Watcher moved to Blaster and stared at the ground. "This was where I fought the first wolf. It pulled Needle from my hand, leaving me without any weapons." He glanced at his companions, then turned his gaze to Planter. "To tell the truth, a voice told me to use the Gauntlets of Life." He held his left hand up in the air, showing the Gauntlets. "I think the voice came from Needle." The sword glowed in his hand.

"Your sword talked to you?" Blaster asked skeptically.

Watcher nodded. "Like I said, there is a presence of

some kind living within the Flail of Regrets, and now I think there's one in Needle as well." He looked straight at Planter. "You felt it before; the way Needle seems to know what to do in battle. It's almost as if it moves on its own."

Planter nodded.

"I think there's some kind of life force trapped within the blade." Watcher put away the sword. "It's probably true about the Gauntlets as well. Maybe that's how the wizards made these powerful weapons—by trapping part of their magical powers within the items."

"That is a great theory, but I don't really care about that right now." Planter scowled at him. "Look what your use of those gauntlets did to the surface of Minecraft. They turned the grass and soil and trees into lifeless stone. Those enchanted weapons have no regard for living things. They're dangerous, just like all magic."

"Well, I'm glad Watcher had those gauntlets," Blaster said. "Those direwolves are pretty tough. I don't know if we could have handled all five without Watcher's purple lightning."

Planter scowled at him. "Maybe you're right, but look what it did to the land. It'll forever be lifeless, just like that petrified village and the dead forest of ash. Magic is reckless and should never be trusted. We'd be better off with all this magic gone from Minecraft."

"What are you saying?" Watcher asked. "You think I should be gone?"

"Well . . . no, of course I don't mean that," Planter said, shaking her head.

"That's kinda what you said." Watcher took a step toward her, but she backed away.

He glanced down at his glowing arms and knew magic was now a part of his life. It wouldn't be possible just to get rid of it; that would be like trying to get rid of an arm or leg. This was who he was. Would magic always be a barrier between them?

Will I ever be close to Planter again? An overwhelming

sadness enveloped Watcher, making him feel lost, adrift in an ocean of despair.

"Well, I'm glad you had the new little trick," Blaster said.

"Me too," Cutter added. "Those wolves are fast and tough . . . and now there are only three of them left." The big warrior smiled. "Three, we can handle, I think."

"The Broken Eight still remain," Er-Lan said.

"As well as the wither king," Mapper added.

"I get it; there are still lots of monsters out there, trying to destroy us," Blaster said. "But with Watcher's new abilities, we have a real advantage. If it costs turning some grass and trees to stone, then who cares? We need to stop Krael from releasing his army of withers. If we fail, no amount of magic is gonna stop hundreds of withers."

"I agree," Cutter said. "We take advantage of Watcher's . . . what'd you call them?"

"They're called the Gauntlets of Life," Watcher said.

"More like the Siphons of Life," Planter added.

Watcher sighed and glanced at her, but she looked away.

"Who cares what they're called?" Fencer said. "As long as they destroy monsters."

"That's the first thing you've said that I like," Blaster said.

Fencer smiled.

"Enough talk!" Watcher snapped. "It's time to move. Mapper, lead us to the Cave of Slumber. We absolutely must be there before Krael and the Broken Eight. No doubt the wolves will head back to their masters, and then they'll know we're still alive." He cast his gaze across their company. "This has just become a race, and being in second place could be fatal." He glanced at Mapper. "Let's go."

The old man pointed a little west of north, and Watcher took off running through the forest, the rest of his companions following.

CHAPTER 26

Krael floated across the desolate landscape, the hills of charred grass and groups of petrified trees a reminder of the epic battle that had once raged across this world . . . the wither king thought it was beautiful.

Glancing over his ashen shoulder, the left skull checked on the Broken Eight; he didn't trust the ancient zombie warriors.

"They stopped," Left said.

The wither king stopped moving and floated up into the air in case there were any threats on the ground. He turned and glared down at the zombie warriors.

"Why have you stopped?" Center asked. "We need to get to the Cave of Slumber before the wizard and his friends reach it."

"Wait . . . the direwolves return, but there is something wrong." Ya-Sik moved to the other zombies and stood in line, their gold armor sparkling in the moonlight; they cast long shadows across the baked and lifeless ground as the moon slowly set behind the western horizon. Suddenly, the zombies' animal-shaped helmets seemed to burst into flames as the rising sun shone its harsh rays upon the landscape.

Two of the zombies suddenly slouched as if they had been somehow wounded or defeated.

"What's wrong with them?" Right asked, gesturing to the dejected warriors.

"Some of the wolves do not return," one of the zombie warriors said.

"How can that be?" Center sounded angry. "They were told to harass the wizard, not have an all-out battle."

"I thought you zombies had some control over these wolves." Left glared down at Ya-Sik.

"The wolves can choose, just like every other living creature. They are not slaves, they are companions, and some have paid dearly for inflicting damage upon our enemy." Ya-Sik's eyes filled with rage as he glared back at the offending wither skull.

The zombies turned toward the east and scanned the bleak terrain for the direwolves. With the sun rising, the reddish early morning light made the furry animals easy to spot.

"The wolves are there." Ra-Sik pointed with his golden short sword.

The other zombies turned to look where their comrade indicated. In the distance, three direwolves appeared from behind an ashen hill of burned grass and charred trees. The once-majestic animals did not walk with their normal air of superiority. Instead, the furry white animals limped and grimaced, their fur ragged and scorched in places. They were soaked in sweat, and their HP was so low, they were near death.

The zombies stepped forward and offered the wolves bones and pieces of meat to eliminate their hunger. Once sated, their HP began to regenerate, bringing them back to their majestic and ferocious state, their fur once more white as a fresh snowfall, something this landscape hadn't seen for a few centuries.

"They killed two of the direwolves; only three remain," Tu-Sik growled, his creeper-head helmet seeming to glare along with the zombie up at the wither. "The wizard and villagers must be made to pay for this atrocity."

"Yes, yes, they will pay, but first we must find the Cave of Slumber and release my army. Think of the destruction that can be brought upon the wizard and his foolish friends when a hundred withers descend upon them."

Ya-Sik took a step toward the wither and drew his golden blade, the magical enchantment pulsing as if it were synchronized with the zombie's heartbeat. "Revenge must be had now . . . not later. The Broken Eight demand restitution. The direwolves are linked to their zombie companions. Each of the Eight can feel the presence of their direwolf, and for one to be killed, it is like having a missing arm or leg; they are forever incomplete." Ya-Sik turned and pointed at the other zombie warriors. "The boy-wizard and his companions must be destroyed . . . now! The Broken Eight will go and do this thing with or without Krael." Ya-Sik took a step closer to Krael, causing the wither to float higher into the air. "After that, perhaps the Broken Eight will go back to the Far Lands and just leave the king of the withers to his slumbering army."

"No! I need your help. I can't go into the Cave without falling asleep," Krael said. "Only one of the Eight can do that."

"Then it would be best if Krael did as suggested, and help us attack the wizard and his friends."

Left scowled at the zombie, but Right gave him a sympathetic look. All three wither skulls could see the pain etched into the faces of the zombies who had lost their wolves. Center and Right felt for the monsters . . . Left, of course, didn't care about anyone other than himself.

Center sighed. "Very well. We will attack the wizard, though it would be easier if we had an army of withers at our backs. Who knows what kind of tricks the wizard might have?"

"The Broken Eight will attack now," the zombie commander said.

"You mean the Broken Six," Left said with a toothy grin.

"Left, be quiet," Center snapped, then brought his gaze back to the zombie. "Very well, we will attack. If your direwolves have regained their strength, have them lead us to the wizard. We'll check their position, then formulate an attack plan. But let me be clear: we won't attack until we have a viable plan." Krael stared down at Ya-Sik. "Agreed?"

The zombie nodded.

"Very well. Tell your direwolves to head out. We're hunting a wizard."

CHAPTER 27

Watcher glanced nervously at Planter as he ran through the thinning forest. Her anger toward anything magical had wounded him deeply, driving spikes of fear into his heart.

I might have lost her, he thought. *What do I do? I can't just decide not to have magic anymore . . . it's part of who I am.*

Watcher stared at the ground as he ran. The rest of the company felt the uneasy tension between the two and remained silent, even Fencer. No one commented on the thinning of the forest or the thick, knee-high grass. Their legs *swooshed* through the verdant blades, the sound like a farmer's scythe cutting through tall stalks of wheat.

Most of the NPCs stayed close to Watcher; the iridescent glow from his arms making holes in the ground easier to spot, but Planter stayed conspicuously out of the lavender light. It was clear she wanted nothing to do with his magic. It made Watcher sad.

The moon had risen and was casting a silvery light upon the landscape. Shadows from the tall blades of grass gave the world a striped appearance. At times, clusters of shadows resembled strangely shaped monsters that would have been unimaginable in the Far Lands . . . but in this world, anything seemed possible.

Gradually, all of the trees disappeared, leaving a wide-open grassy plain.

"This almost seems normal," Blaster said as he put on his black leather armor. His body instantly merged with the darkness. "You'd think we were on the plains in the Far Lands."

"That's what I was thinking," Cutter said. "I wouldn't mind coming across a horse or two."

"There's something up ahead." Watcher pointed to the dark horizon, his glowing arms casting enough light for the party to see.

"What do you see?" Mapper asked.

Watcher focused his attention on the horizon. "I see some tall columns of . . . something, but I can't be sure what they are at this distance. They look really tall and really wide."

"Maybe they're columns around the entrance to the Cave of Slumber," Planter said.

Mapper fumbled with his inventory, then pulled out his map. He held it close to Watcher's shoulder, using the magical purple glow to get a better look. "No, it can't be that. We're too far from the Cave to see its entrance yet."

"Then what do you think it is?" Watcher asked. "Do you see anything on the map?"

"It just shows a bunch of large dots, but there's no name or description . . ." Mapper sounded perplexed. "I have no idea what it is."

"Great, an unknown structure, completely unlike anything we've ever seen, in the middle of the night, in a world ravaged by the magic of the NPC wizards and monster warlocks . . . do I have it right?" Blaster smiled, his shining teeth standing out in the darkness.

"That sounds about right," Watcher said.

Blaster nodded, then drew his two curved knives. "Then let's move faster and get this little surprise over with."

"I agree. Let's do this!" Cutter yelled as he drew his diamond sword.

The two NPCs shifted into a sprint, the rest of the villagers following suit. They moved as fast as they could, occasionally resting to refuel with a loaf of bread or piece of steak, keeping their hunger down and their HP up. After a couple of hours of running, the moon now past its zenith, they finally reached the strange-looking structures.

All throughout the strange biome, huge cylinders of stone stuck up through the tall grass. They were a dozen blocks in diameter and probably thirty blocks tall, if not more. It was as if something had shot the stone columns up out of the ground, like nails through a thin piece of wood. Watcher saw caves dug into the bases of the structures, each dark and foreboding. Moonlight filled some of the caverns, revealing passages extending deep underground. Maybe it was his imagination, but Watcher thought he saw movement within some of them.

"I'm not very excited about finding out what's inside those caves," he whispered.

"Er-Lan agrees," the zombie replied softly. "Perhaps it could be . . . oh no."

"What's wrong?" Planter asked.

"The Eight are near; Er-Lan can feel them." The zombie glanced around at the dark caves and tall, rocky columns. "All must go quickly . . . now." Er-Lan moved away faster than Watcher had ever seen, sprinting through the grass as if he had just drunk a potion of swiftness.

They darted through the biome, weaving their way around the tall columns of stone. Er-Lan's body parted the grass, his clawed feet easily trampling the tall blades and occasional shrubs. An expression of panic covered his scarred face as his eyes darted to the left and right, searching for their unseen pursuers.

"Er-Lan, are you sure—the Broken Eight are—out there?" Watcher asked between strained breaths.

"Er-Lan can feel them," the zombie said. "They draw near."

"But how can you know that they're—"

A growl cut through the swishing of legs in the grass and the stomping of booted feet on the ground. It was a sound every one of the NPCs knew by now, as evidenced by the expressions of fear on their square faces.

"Direwolves," Er-Lan hissed.

"Everyone, draw bows," Watcher said in a loud voice.

"Shhh . . ." Fencer whispered. "They'll hear you and know where we are."

"They already know where we are," Watcher said. "The question is . . . will they catch us before we reach the Cave?" He glanced at Mapper. "How much longer?"

Mapper pulled out the map as he ran, then fumbled with it; the parchment came loose from his grasp and drifted into the air.

Fortunately, Blaster was right behind the old man. He snatched the map out of the air and handed it back to him.

"Here you go," Blaster said with a smile.

"Thanks." Mapper looked embarrassed. He glanced down at the map, turned it so it was facing north, then glanced at their surroundings. "We should arrive at the Cave of Slumber by dawn."

Watcher glanced up at the moon, then checked the eastern horizon; it was still as dark as coal. "Dawn is a long way away."

Another angry howl cut through the air.

"Seems like an eternity," Blaster said, no smile on his face now.

"Yep." Watcher nodded.

Just then, a set of glowing red eyes appeared in the darkness to the left. Watcher fired an arrow at the tiny points of light, but they quickly disappeared.

"Everyone, watch our flanks," Watcher said. "The direwolves are out there."

"This doesn't seem right." Planter took a breath and continued. "It seems like they're driving us toward something."

"Yeah, I agree," Cutter said.

Watcher glanced at Planter, then suddenly knew what to do. "Planter, fire arrows up ahead. Let's see what's out there."

She nodded, then nocked an arrow and pulled back the string. When she released it, the arrow instantly burst into fiery life, the flaming shaft creating a halo of light as it streaked through the air. It landed on the ground up ahead, revealing more tall grass, though the stone cylinders were beginning to dwindle.

"More arrows," Watcher said.

She fired again and again as they ran, the flaming arrows streaking through the dark sky like meteors from the heavens. They landed in the tall grass, the magical flames staying wrapped around the pointed shafts and not spreading to the grass. More and more of the landscape was revealed as they moved forward, but they still saw no zombie warriors.

"More . . . more."

She fired continually, the *Infinity* enchantment making it impossible to run out of arrows. The shafts streaked through the air, revealing the same scene over and over, until the faintest flicker of gold appeared in the distance.

"Everyone stop!" Watcher skidded to a stop and crouched down in the grass. "Watch our flanks and rear for wolves."

Warriors took up positions around their formation, scared eyes scanning the darkness for attackers.

Watcher pulled out a fire arrow from his inventory and fitted it to his bow. He pulled the bowstring back as far as possible, then let loose. The arrow flew high into the air, making a graceful arc into the night sky, then came down to land in the grass right at the feet of a zombie warrior, a shimmering gold helmet in the shape of a dragon's head on the monster's head.

"The Eight," Er-Lan moaned, terrified.

"They're between us and the Cave of Slumber," Mapper said. "They beat us here."

"We have to get past them somehow and block them from entering the Cave," Watcher said.

"That's a great goal, but do you have an idea for how to do it?" Blaster asked.

Watcher glanced at Planter and sighed. "Yeah . . . but none of you are gonna like it."

"It's better than just standing here and waiting for them to attack us," Cutter said.

"So, what's your plan?" Mapper asked.

Watcher put away his bow, then glanced at his friends, a look of grim determination on his square face.

"My idea is this: CHARGE!"

Watcher sprinted straight for the monsters, yelling at the top of his lungs. The other NPCs, surprised for just an instant, all drew their swords and followed the young boy, their battle cries filling the air, while ahead the Broken Eight closed ranks, drew their enchanted swords and shields, and waited for their prey to come to them.

CHAPTER 28

Fury and rage filled Watcher's mind as he streaked through the tall grass toward the line of zombies. The Broken Eight stood next to each other, the six ancient zombie warriors holding their spiked shields in their left hands and glowing iron short swords in their right. They looked menacing in their enchanted gold armor, each with a ferocious monster-head helmet staring at their attackers.

Magical power built within Watcher as his diamond boots hammered the ground. He could hear his friends behind him, but his attention was completely focused on his magic . . . and his targets. Gathering his powers, he held his arms before him. The Gauntlets of Life flashed bright, then threw bolts of purple lightning at the zombies, striking their shields.

The soil and grass under Watcher's feet grew cold as the ancient relic drew power from the ground beneath his feet. The dirt became rock hard as the blades of grass petrified into thin slivers of stone. The stony-grass cracked and shattered under the feet of his companions, sounding like broken glass.

Watcher threw more bolts of lightning, focusing his power on the center of the line. The sparkling shafts of power crackled across the zombies' bodies and shields, their faces grimacing in pain. He blasted them again and again, the Gauntlets forming large circles of stone around his feet. The energy slammed into the zombies, knocking two of them to the ground, while others staggered backwards.

Watcher continued the assault as he drew closer, slamming his magic into the monsters at the center of the line. Arrows zipped through the air and struck the zombies, most of the shafts just bouncing off their armor, but a few slipped between gold plates and found green zombie-flesh.

Finally, the center buckled and the zombies fell backward to the ground. Their comrades dragged the fallen away just as Watcher reached their lines.

In a flash, he had the Flail of Regrets in his hand. He swung the enchanted weapon with all his might. The chain extended, reaching out to the closest zombie. The monster brought up his shield, but it already showed cracks from the earlier magical assault. The curved shield shattered, the spiked cube of the flail smashing into the creature's chest, making the zombie flash red as it took damage. Watcher yanked the Flail free, then struck the zombie one more time. The spiked cube smashed into the monster's helmet, making the zombie flash red as the last of the ancient creature's HP was torn from its body. It fell to the ground, then disappeared as Watcher ran through the zombie ranks, the rest of his friends following.

The zombies screamed in rage and ran to their fallen comrades as the NPCs streaked past them through the night. Watcher slowed for a moment and glanced at his companions. No one was missing . . . good.

"Mapper . . . where's Mapper?" Watcher shouted.

"Here I am." The old man was at the rear of the company, running next to Fencer.

"Mapper, lead everyone to the Cave of Slumber," Watcher said. "Blaster, Cutter and I will take up the rear and make sure the zombies don't attack."

"You aren't doing that without me," Planter said, a stern expression on her square face. "Someone needs to be there to keep you three out of trouble."

"Great, we could use your bow." Watcher smiled. "Mapper . . . go!"

The old man sprinted forward, following the map, the remaining NPC warriors following him. Behind them, Watcher and his friends slowly walked backward, watching for a counterattack.

"Okay, genius," Blaster said. "How are we going to find the Cave without the map?"

"I can feel its pull," Watcher said.

Planter nodded in agreement.

That's strange, he thought.

They moved through the high grass, the sounds of Mapper and the others fading into the night. Eventually, they turned and ran, following the trail of crushed grass, but after a dozen blocks, the landscape changed from grassy plains into a desert. Footprints could be seen in the sand, marking where Mapper and the others had run.

"At least this desert hasn't been melted into glass," Cutter said.

"Not yet, anyway," Planter added with a glance toward Watcher.

They continued backwards across the sands, watching out for pursuers, as the sun started to peek up from behind the eastern horizon. The sky became a wash of pale reds and oranges as dawn spread across the landscape, adding much-needed color to the pallid landscape.

"Look." Cutter pointed back toward the grassland.

Five gold-clad zombie warriors emerged from the dark grass with three wolves on their right flank. They walked slowly toward the villagers, looks of rage and determination on their square faces. Floating above them was Krael, the king of the withers, the two golden Crowns of Skulls shining bright on his heads in the rosy dawn light.

"You have come to the end of your days, boy!" Krael shouted. "My zombies will feast on your XP, and then my wither army will cover the lands of Minecraft with misery and grief."

Watcher and the others said nothing. They just continued to walk backward, ready and waiting for the attack to come.

"I can see the entrance to the Cave of Slumber," Planter said in a low voice. "I think we should make a run for it."

"Maybe you're right," Watcher said as he continued to move backward. "Here's what I want to do. Cutter, you and Blaster—"

"Here's a little gift, wizard!" Krael yelled, launching a volley of flaming skulls at the four NPCs.

"Forget the plan," Watcher said. "Run!"

They turned and ran, the dark skulls exploding on the ground behind them, carving a huge crater into the ground.

Ahead, Mapper stood next to a tunnel entrance carved into the side of a huge mountain of sand and sandstone.

"Hurry . . . hurry!" the old NPC shouted.

Watcher sprinted across the sands, his friends running ahead of him. He put away the Flail of Regrets and drew Needle in case he needed to bat away a flaming skull. A huge explosion rocked the landscape, causing cubes of sand to shift around him, but the mountain before him held steady. Around the mountain, the blocks of sand and sandstone shimmered with a purple luminescence; clearly, they were protected by some kind of enchantment.

"Hurry . . . he's firing again!" Mapper shouted.

Watcher turned just as Krael launched another barrage of flaming skulls, one of them heading right at Watcher. Fear shot down every nerve, making him shiver with fright.

Relax and knock them away, a voice said in his mind.

Is that you, Needle? Watcher thought.

Just stop and relax, the voice said.

Stopping his retreat, Watcher turned and faced the skulls heading straight for him.

"Watcher, what are you doing?" Planter shouted behind him. "Run!"

Taking a deep breath, Watcher tried to relax, even though he had an overwhelming urge to turn and flee. But instead, he trusted the voice in his head and focused on the wither king's attack.

The skulls were getting closer . . . and closer . . . and closer, until . . .

Needle suddenly moved on its own, forcing the muscles in Watcher's arm to react as the magical blade struck out at the flaming skulls, deflecting the three projectiles with such speed, the sword was just a blur. It ricocheted each skull back toward the zombies' right flank, directly at the remaining direwolves. The flaming skulls exploded when they hit the ground, enveloping the animals in a mighty blast, destroying two of them, leaving only one alive.

Now . . . RUN! the voice shouted in Watcher's mind.

Watcher turned and fled to the entrance of the Cave of Slumber, the bloodthirsty surviving members of the Broken Eight and the enraged king of the withers right on his heels.

CHAPTER 29

They sprinted through the passage, terrifying snarls and moans filling the air behind them. Light from Watcher's glowing arms and shoulders lit the passage with a lavender hue, giving the villagers just enough light to see the ground. They should have been watching for pressure plates, trip wires, and other traps, but fear now controlled the NPCs.

Watcher glanced over his shoulder, expecting a golden zombie or flaming skull to enter the passage after them, but so far it was empty save for his friends. Blaster followed him, the boy's dark armor making him difficult to see. The entrance to the tunnel was now dark, as the walls of the corridor were free from any enchantments like those on the mountainside. If the wither fired one of his flaming skulls into the passage, he could cause the entire tunnel to collapse under an avalanche of sand and gravel; they had to be careful.

Suddenly, Watcher collided with the sandy wall. He hadn't noticed the passage turned to the right.

"Maybe avoid walking into the walls," Blaster said with a grin.

"I was watching for the monsters."

Blaster nodded and helped his friend to his feet. "I

blocked off the tunnel with some stone. It should give us a little time to prepare."

"Prepare for what?" Watcher asked.

"It seems this is gonna be our last stand." Blaster put a hand on Watcher's shoulder. "Either we're walking out of this passage or an army of withers is; I don't see another option. We need to be prepared for the battle that's coming."

Watcher nodded, then followed as Blaster sprinted through the winding, descending tunnel. Eventually, Watcher could see the end of the sandy hallway. Warm yellow light filled the opening, but not the flickering kind from a torch or fireplace; this was a constant source, unwavering for centuries.

When he reached the corridor's end, Watcher was shocked by what he found. The tunnel spilled into a massive room shaped like a huge cylinder. It must have been at least thirty blocks across, its ceiling easily two dozen blocks high. It looked like some kind of meeting hall or assembly area.

"Maybe it was the place where the wizards stayed while they were constructing the Cave," someone said in awe.

Watcher glanced at the voice and found Mapper staring at the surroundings, a look of wonder on his wrinkled face. Everything around them was white, with the walls, floor, and ceiling constructed from blocks of pristine quartz. Redstone lanterns mounted to the ceiling bathed the room in a warm yellow light. Across the floor and walls, embedded redstone blocks created complex geometric patterns, with a great spiral on the floor turning from the walls to the center of the chamber. It was fantastic.

Brewing stands and crafting benches stood along one wall with a line of furnaces on either side, although no fires burned in the furnaces, their surfaces having gone cold many centuries ago. On another wall, tall shelves of books surrounded enchantment tables. A book sat open on a black-and-red table, the pages leafing back and forth on their own. Tiny letters floated from the book to the table, adding magical power to the enchantments.

A howl suddenly sliced through the circular chamber. Tiny, square goosebumps formed on Watcher's arms when a vicious moan was soon added to the wolf's angry voice. Pounding footsteps echoed through the passage as more growling moans filled the chamber.

"Build some defenses, fast!" Cutter set blocks of stone on the ground, forming a barricade across the center of the room. The others did the same, adding their blocks to those Cutter was hurriedly placing on the ground.

Watcher glanced around at their surroundings, then stared down at the Gauntlets of Life. There was nothing alive in this chamber; all the blocks were inert. That meant the Gauntlets of Life would offer no aid in their hour of need.

"Then we'll just have to do this on our own," Watcher whispered to himself.

He glanced around the room, looking for anything that might help them, like some ancient artifact or weapon yet to be used. But there was nothing but bookcases, crafting tables and brewing stations.

The howl and moans were getting louder.

And then he saw it: another passage leading out of the room. It was a wide tunnel, four blocks wide and six high.

I bet that leads to the Cave of Slumber, Watcher thought.

Running to the tunnel, he sprinted through the dark passage, the enchantments pulsing through his body lighting the walls and floor. The corridor smelled musty and old, as if it had been empty for centuries. Dust kicked up into the air as he ran, tickling his nose and making him cough. The corridor angled upward as it burrowed through the mountain of sand and sandstone until it finally ended. And what it revealed was shocking.

Before him was a gigantic, perfectly spherical chamber; it was the Cave of Slumber. The walls of the Cave sparkled with a purple glow; clearly, they were enchanted, probably to make escape impossible. Other tunnels could be seen piercing the sides of the Cave, each leading into the chamber from somewhere different. Redstone lanterns floated in the air all throughout the cave, each atop a redstone block that floated on nothing; the rules of physics didn't apply in Minecraft.

The light from the redstone lanterns illuminated a sea of withers that hovered in the air, each motionless, their three skulls leaning to the side, as if they were asleep. There were hundreds of them, each identical in appearance; this was Krael's wither army.

"The king of the withers cannot be allowed to have this army," Watcher whispered to the silent chamber.

The withers were not spread out evenly in the chamber. In fact, it seemed as if the monsters had been flying toward the far side of the cave, trying to reach something, when they fell asleep and froze in place.

And then he saw it. A sparkling gold thing sat on the far side of the Cave atop a pedestal made of sandstone. Watcher took a step into the cave to try to get a better look, and instantly, he started feeling fatigued, the longing thought of a blissful sleep growing in his mind. As quickly as he could, he stepped back, realizing the magic of the cave had started acting on him.

Far behind him, someone yelled, their pain-filled voice echoing up through the passage and into the Cave of Slumber. The pinging sound of arrows bouncing off shields followed the shout; the zombies had made it into the quartz chamber.

"I have to get back to my friends."

The sounds of fighting echoed through the passage. But before he turned, Watcher found his eyes drawn again to that iridescent thing on the other side of the chamber. The gold artifact shone brightly, but this time he could also see tiny black objects around the top.

And then a realization dawned on him: it was the third Crown of Skulls.

If Krael gets that artifact, then his power may become unlimited, voices said within his mind. In fact, he realized, it was three voices all speaking at once, likely from the Flail, Needle, and the Gauntlets of Power.

Watcher could feel the three artifacts agreeing.

"I have to get that before the wither does." Someone shouted in pain again behind him. "But first I have to check on my friends."

Turning, he sprinted back through the sandstone tunnel and entered the quartz chamber. Near the opposite wall, the zombie warriors were trying to enter the chamber, but the other NPCs were flooding the entrance with arrows; the Eight couldn't take a step into the room without being hit by a dozen arrows at the same time. He doubted any of the zombies or the lone direwolf would survive that, which gave the villagers a little time, but only until they ran out of arrows.

Glancing around the room, he found Blaster and ran to him. "Blaster, I found the Cave of Slumber."

"That's really great, but how about you help us out here? Do your magic thing," Blaster said.

Watcher wanted to reach into his inventory and draw the Bow of Destruction, but then a plan materialized in his head.

"Blaster, I have an idea, but you'll need to trust me . . . everyone will need to trust me."

Blaster glanced at his friend between shots. "OK, what do you need us to do?"

He motioned for Planter to come to his side, and then he explained his plan to the two of them. Blaster grinned, then ran off to tell the others.

"Are you with me?" Watcher asked Planter.

She nodded, but when her eyes fell upon the Gauntlets of Life, she scowled, then nodded again.

"OK, then, come with me," Watcher said. "We'll get only one shot, so we need to make it a good one."

Watcher and Planter moved to the side of the room and prepared their trap, both knowing that if they messed this up, they were all doomed.

CHAPTER 30

Watcher and Planter moved to the side of the chamber and positioned themselves out of sight behind a set of bookshelves while all the other NPCs continued to fire at the entrance, keeping the zombies back.

Drawing the Fossil Bow of Destruction from his inventory, Watcher waved it to Blaster, who nodded and gave Watcher a grin.

"I'm running out of arrows," Blaster said loudly as he ducked behind the cobblestone defensive wall. "Does anyone have any?"

"I'm out too," Cutter shouted.

The villagers all stopped firing and hid behind their barricades with more declarations of running out of arrows.

A vile laugh floated from the passage. It was a scratchy, hacking sound that was joined by two others, one booming, the other lyrical and smooth. They brought chills to Watcher's soul. He knew those voices; it was Krael, the king of the withers.

"It seems you've run out of arrows." The monster laughed. "Zombies, move forward."

The five remaining members of the Broken Eight stepped into the chamber and formed a line, as if daring the NPCs to charge. No one moved, the villagers remaining hidden behind their cobblestone wall. With the sole surviving direwolf behind them, the zombie warriors moved forward, slowly advancing on the NPCs' position.

A feeling of fear spread through the room as if it were an infectious disease; all of the NPCs completely were terrified of these monsters. They'd lost many friends already to their swords and fangs, and no one wanted to be next.

"Hurry . . . do something before—" a villager shouted. Someone put their hand over the scared NPC's mouth, silencing his yells.

Krael's laughter suddenly stopped. Watcher wanted to peer out from behind the bookcase to see what was happening, but he didn't dare give away his position. Instead, he drew back on the Bow of Destruction, and an arrow automatically appeared on the string, its shaft glistening with magical power. The enchanted weapon reached out to Watcher's HP, searching for power. He grunted as he flashed red, but glanced at Planter and shook his head. She had a splash potion of healing ready to use on him, but she waited until he gave the signal.

"I can feel your presence, wizard. You're not as clever as you think." Krael laughed again, then fired a barrage of flaming skulls.

The first skull slammed into the bookcase, shredding it to splinters, then the second one hit Watcher just as he released the bowstring and fired at the closest zombie. The arrow from the Fossil Bow of Destruction leaped off the string and struck the monster, passing right through his golden armor as if it were made of paper. The zombie screamed, his pain and surprise filling the chamber, then disappeared as a third flaming skull struck Watcher, knocking him to the ground. Gray spirals floated around his head as the wither effect permeated his body; he could no longer tell how much HP he had. He tried to stand, but his legs buckled under him and he fell back to the floor, severely wounded. He dropped the Bow as he struggled to stand, but lacked the strength.

"There is the wizard," Center said, Left and Right grinning. "Zombies, destroy him!"

A sense of helplessness spread through Watcher. He was too weak to stand, and he couldn't protect Planter . . . they were doomed.

But then, Planter did something that caused him to scream out in horror: she picked up the Bow and pulled back on the string. A flash of red light covered her body as the Bow demanded its HP price. Screaming in pain, she fired the bow. The arrow streaked through the air and missed the direwolf, embedding itself into the wall, then disappeared. The animal growled angrily.

Watcher reached into his inventory and found a potion of healing. He knew it wouldn't do any good, but he threw the splash potion on Planter anyway. The liquid hit her and splashed onto him too, giving Watcher a little more strength. But the strangest thing was, it seemed to help Planter as well, even though she was using the Bow.

Watcher glanced at the zombies; they were still in a line, advancing across the room. "Aim for the last zombie." Watcher's voice was weak. He summoned all his strength. "Aim for the last zombie before it's too late."

Planter glanced down at him as another wave of torture crashed down upon her. With an agonized scream, she fell to one knee, but still nodded her head in understanding. She pulled the string back again, causing another arrow to appear, and aimed at the farthest zombie, then closed her eyes and concentrated; the iridescent glow from the bow seemed to leak into Planter, making her glow as well. And then she released.

The glistening arrow streaked through the chamber, heading for the farthest zombie. But, unfortunately for the rest of the zombies, the other Broken Eight were directly in its path. The magical projectile passed through the first zombie, then went through the next and the next, taking their HP with it. The glistening shaft missed one of the monsters, just wounding it in the shoulder, but still continued to the last zombie . . . its target. The magical arrow struck the ancient warrior in the chest, taking the last of the creature's HP.

The zombies stood there for a moment, sheer disbelief on their scarred faces, and then, one after another, they fell to their knees and collapsed as the magical power in the arrow from the Fossil Bow of Destruction did its work. The lone surviving zombie slowly stood, badly wounded, then fled from the chamber and disappeared into the dark passage.

The Broken Eight were no more.

"She did it!" Blaster screamed . . . and then he realized what she had done. "Healing potions! She needs healing potions!"

But Watcher knew it wouldn't do any good. Planter wasn't a wizard or the descendant of a wizard. She had no magical powers to protect her from the ravages of the Bow of Destruction; she'd never be able to let go of it until it had taken all her HP. He took her up in his arms as the rest of the NPCs attacked the surviving direwolf.

"Planter, what did you do?" Tears trickled down Watcher's square face. "You shouldn't have used the bow."

"I realized that the most important thing to me was about to be destroyed . . ." she coughed, "and I couldn't allow that to happen."

"But the Bow! You picked up the Bow of Destruction. You know what that means."

Another wave of pain crashed down upon Planter as she flashed red, taking damage. She looked at the bow sadly, but then a puzzled expression came across her face. And then she did the most amazing thing Watcher had ever seen: she released the Fossil Bow of Destruction, the ancient weapon just clattering to the ground.

"Planter . . . what happened?"

"I don't know, but maybe we finish this battle and figure it out later. There's still a wither out there that needs to be destroyed; it's time to fight."

"Absolutely." Watcher stood, the Flail of Regrets in his hand, his eyes burning with rage as he faced the dark passage, ready to do battle with his enemy, Krael, the king of the withers.

CHAPTER 31

A scream of rage echoed out of the dark tunnel. "You destroyed my zombies . . . MY ZOMBIES!" Krael was in a fury. The wither was still in the passage, unwilling to come out and be a target, for now. But Watcher knew he still had to come out and try to rescue his wither army.

"Blaster, come here," Watcher said as he handed a loaf of bread to Planter. Her health was slowly returning.

"What?" Blaster asked.

"I have a plan for the wither, but need your help," Watcher said. "You think you could blow something up for me?"

A huge grin spread across Blaster's square face at the thought.

"I need both of you to help." Watcher glanced at Planter, then Blaster. They both nodded. "Here's my plan."

Watcher explained what he was going to do. As he spoke, Blaster's smile just grew larger, but the expression on Planter's face was one of fear.

"This is dangerous," she said.

"I know." Watcher grabbed her hand and held it; she didn't pull away. "But it's the only way. With those two

Crowns of Skulls on the wither, he may be impossible to defeat . . . this is the only way."

She nodded.

"Ok . . . ready?" Watcher picked up the Bow of Destruction and put it in his inventory, then got ready to run. Meanwhile, Blaster waved his bow in the air, then aimed an arrow at the tunnel entrance. The other villagers lifted their bows and drew arrows.

"Now!"

Watcher raced for the tunnel leading to the Cave of Slumber. At the same time, the villagers all fired. A hail of arrows flew toward the tunnel, but at the same time, a stream of flaming skulls blasted from it through the chamber, striking the cobblestone wall and blowing it to bits. Villagers flew through the air as more skulls hammered their defenses.

Watcher bolted across the quartz chamber as he drank a potion of leaping. He could hear the screams of pain and fear from his comrades, but he couldn't focus on them. He had to get into the Cave of Slumber and steal the third Crown of Skulls before Krael realized it was there.

"Blaster, just follow the plan," Watcher shouted over his shoulder. "I'll give the word when it's time."

He ran into the passage just as Krael emerged from the opposite tunnel. The wither had a sparkling shield around his body, which all withers could create, protecting them from arrows, but which stopped them from firing their flaming skulls. Watcher took advantage of it and ran as fast as he could, not bothering to weave back and forth to make himself difficult to hit.

The wither saw Watcher and screamed in fury. As Watcher ran, he could hear shouts of pain as the monster injured some of the villagers, but in seconds, a scream of rage echoed through the passage behind him; Krael was in the tunnel and chasing him . . . perfect.

Watcher sprinted into the Cave of Slumber and leaped onto the first redstone block, then jumped onto an unconscious wither. The creature bobbed up and down just a bit under his weight. Watcher continued, jumping to the next wither, leaping to a nearby redstone lantern, then repeating the process. It was like the hardest and most deadly parkour course ever devised. The bottom of the cave was cloaked in darkness and likely a far way down; a fall would probably be fatal.

The sound of digging echoed through the cavern; Blaster was starting the next part of the plan . . . good. Watcher was tempted to glance over his shoulder to see the progress, but he didn't dare; the slightest misstep would be lethal.

A great roar filled the chamber as Krael entered the Cave of Slumber.

"We will destroy you, wizard!" the three skulls screeched in unison.

Watcher prepared for a blast of flaming skulls, but no attack came. Likely, Krael didn't want to hit any of the other withers floating in the cavern.

He jumped from creature to lantern again and again as an overwhelming urge to take a nap invaded his mind; the magic enchantments that enveloped the Cave of Slumber were taking effect. If he didn't hurry, he'd likely be trapped here.

Out of the corner of his eye, Watcher spotted the king of the withers. He was floating toward the Crown of Skulls; he'd spotted it and was trying to reach it first. This had become a race and coming in second would not be good. He tried to move faster, but fatigue and sleepiness were making his legs feel leaden.

Maybe if I close my eyes for a minute, I can rest and build up some strength. The thought felt like a comfortable blanket, embracing Watcher's body and making his eyes feel heavy.

NO! A voice boomed from within his head; it came from the Flail of Regrets. *If the wither king gets the third Crown of Skulls, he'll be able to awaken his army. KEEP MOVING, OR ALL IS LOST!*

Watcher reached into his inventory and grabbed the weapon. The presence of the magical item whispering to him in the back of his mind pushed back the sleepiness and allowed him to move faster. With the Flail of Regrets in his hand, Watcher sprang from wither to wither, standing on ashen shoulders and dark heads as if they were stepping stones.

The Crown of Skulls was getting closer. There were three more jumps to go, and then he'd reach the magical relic.

"I must reach it before Krael does," Watcher said to himself.

Do it . . . get the Crown. The voice from the Flail of Regrets echoed in his mind. *If the king of the withers gains the third Crown of Skulls, he will rain misery and despair upon the whole of Minecraft.*

"I know, thanks for not adding any pressure."

Watcher gritted his teeth and jumped to the next wither. The monster floated next to a redstone lantern, the patterned cube glowing with an orange luster. Watcher leaped to the lantern, then jumped to the next floating monster. His foot landed on the wither's left head, then slipped off. He stumbled and started to fall.

Fear blasted through his body, every nerve ignited. Reaching out, he managed to hook one of the sharp spikes at the end of the Flail onto the center head of the wither, then yanked, pulling himself back on top of the dark monster's shoulders.

Glancing over his shoulder, Watcher spotted Krael. The wither king was almost to the Crown of Skulls as well, but he was drifting slower and slower.

Sprinting for one step, Watcher jumped to the next redstone lantern, then kept going without a pause, taking the last leap. It was far, easily three blocks, and at an angle; he might not make it. Flying through the air in what felt like slow motion, Watcher saw the sandy platform on which the Crown of Skulls sat getting closer and closer . . . but then he started to fall.

He wasn't going to make it.

Swinging the Flail with all his might, he smashed the spiked cube into a block of sandstone; thankfully, it stuck. Watcher held onto the handle of the weapon with all his strength as his body collided with the sandy wall.

Hanging from the enchanted weapon, Watcher glanced over his shoulder at Krael. The wither saw him and his eyes snapped wide open, sleepiness forgotten.

"You'll never get out of this cavern alive, wizard." The center head glared at him.

Hurry! The voice echoed in his mind.

Watcher climbed the chain connected to the spiked ball, using the Flail of Regrets like a rope. When he reached the sandstone platform, he grabbed the edge and pulled himself up, his strength waning. The thought of sleep seemed to dominate his mind, but Watcher pushed it aside and focused on his task. Pulling the Flail loose from the sandstone, he stuffed it back into his inventory and moved to the glowing pedestal. The Crown of Skulls was right there.

"Don't you dare touch that!" Krael screeched.

Watcher ignored the monster and grabbed the artifact.

"Noooooo!"

Watcher ducked just as a flaming skull flew past his head. Quickly, he removed his diamond chest plate and put it into his inventory.

"You'll never escape, fool!" The king of the withers floated closer, a look of fury in its six eyes.

Watcher glanced at the wither, then pulled out a set of Elytra wings and strapped them to his back. With icy fear pulsing through his veins, Watcher took two quick steps, then jumped off the sandstone platform and plummeted into the Cave of Slumber.

CHAPTER 32

Watcher held his breath and leaned forward, causing the wings to snap open. He started breathing again as they caught the wind and lifted him higher into the air.

Well, I won't fall to my death, he thought. *At least not yet.*

Banking to the left, Watcher narrowly avoided a collision with a wither; it likely would have been a fatal one. He clutched the Crown of Skulls tight in his right hand.

"I'm glad I listened to you, sister, and brought these wings with me," Watcher said to the darkness.

DIVE! The voice from the Flail suddenly boomed through his mind.

Watcher descended just as a flaming skull streaked overhead, barely missing him.

Move faster. If you stay in the Cave of Slumber for too long, you'll fall asleep, and I won't be able to help you.

Watcher nodded, then leaned forward, trading altitude for speed. He streaked through the chamber as fast as possible, banking left and right, dodging sleeping withers and redstone lanterns. The tips of his wings brushed occasionally against the sleeping monsters, making them shudder. His vision blurred slightly as the Cave's spell tried to grasp his mind.

Volleys of flaming skulls rained down upon him, the king of the withers desperate to stop him. The urge to glance over his shoulder to see how close the monster was to him was almost irresistible, but he knew that it was impossible. It took every bit of concentration to keep his speed up while at the same time avoiding all the floating obstacles.

He could see the exit on the other side of the cavern. Blaster, Cutter, and Planter were moving about, placing the last explosives.

Bank left!

He turned to the left just as a flaming skull nicked his boot and slammed into a redstone lantern. The glowing cube shattered into a million shards, the razor-sharp pieces slicing into his skin. He held up the Crown of Skulls, hoping to block some of the shrapnel from hitting him in the face.

Faster . . . faster.

Watcher was so tired he was having a hard time understanding the words. Suddenly, an enraged scream from the wither king gave him the briefest jolt of fear, making him dive to gain speed.

You're too low . . . you'll miss the tunnel, the mystical voice from the Flail sounded desperate. *Pull up!*

Watcher could see the tunnel; the Flail was right. He leaned back and pulled up, slowing down as he climbed. He was only a few seconds from the tunnel now.

"Blaster, light the TNT, NOW!" Watcher's voice sounded like thunder in the gigantic chamber.

Another flaming skull streaked by, smashing into a wither; the deadly projectile ricocheted off the monster and shattered another redstone lantern. More shards of glass flew through the air, bouncing off the Crown of Skulls as Watcher held it over his eyes.

"WIZARD . . . I'M GOING TO DESTROY YOU!" Krael's demonic voice was terrifying.

Watcher pulled in his arms and legs to reduce drag, then leaned forward, accelerating toward the exit tunnel. He could see the blocks of TNT starting to blink; the fuse had been lit, and he had only one chance at this. If he crashed, he would be trapped in the Cave of Slumber.

"I can do this . . . I can do this . . ." Watcher hoped his words would bring him more courage and more speed, but they did neither. The TNT blinked faster, almost ready to explode. He tried to will himself to go faster, but—

Flaming skulls streaked just over his head. The first and second ones barely missed him, but the third slammed into his side, throwing him sideways and knocking the Crown of Skulls from his hand. It tumbled through the air and disappeared into the darkness that shrouded the bottom of the Cave.

"NOOOOOO!" Watcher shouted.

Leave it . . . get out of the Cave before it's too late! The voice of the Flail sounded panicked.

Watcher tucked his arms into his sides and leaned forward, making himself as aerodynamic as possible. He streaked through the air like a living missile, the floating bodies of the withers mere shadowy blurs as he zipped past. He turned left and right, narrowly avoiding them as he sped through the last of the chamber. Pulling up at the last minute, he shot through the tunnel just as the TNT detonated.

Everything became noise and fire and dust and chaos as the blast knocked him to the side, smashing him into one wall of the tunnel, then throwing him against the other. Watcher was battered back and forth, the blast deafening around him. Pain exploded throughout his body as he was crushed by blocks of sand and crashed into walls still standing. A wall of fire seemed to envelop him as he shot through the passage, tumbling out of control until finally, everything grew quiet, and darkness wrapped around him like a funeral shroud.

CHAPTER 33

Watcher's head felt like an anvil being pounded on by a blacksmith's hammer. With every pulse of his heart, pain surged through his skull, making him wish . . .

Wait a minute . . . I'm alive.

"I'm alive!"

Watcher started to sit up, but realized someone was holding him in their arms. Tilting his head back, he gazed up into the most beautiful green eyes he'd ever seen.

"Planter . . . you're okay?"

"I should be the one worried about you," she said, a playful scowl on her face. "You gave us quite the scare."

"What happened?" he asked.

"Well, as near as I can tell," Blaster said, kneeling on the left, "you flew through the tunnel while all the TNT was detonating."

He patted Watcher's shoulder, making him cringe in pain, so Blaster gave him a potion of healing, which he drank.

"But you did a good job flying through the tunnel at the very last moment," Blaster said. "I'm sure most people would have wanted to be a second ahead of the explosion, but you did it just when everything was det-onating . . . nice."

"What about Krael?" Watcher asked. "Did he get out?"

"Look." Planter pointed at the tunnel.

Blocks of sand and gravel choked what was left of the passage entrance. The entire tunnel had been destroyed.

"While you were unconscious, we heard Krael screaming in frustration, but his voice grew softer and softer until we couldn't hear anything," Blaster said. "I'm not very excited about digging through all the debris to find out what really happened to him."

Watcher nodded, then winced as his headache reminded the boy it was still there. "So Krael's gone?"

Blaster nodded.

He glanced up at Planter, and she nodded as well.

A sense of relief spread through Watcher like a wave of cool water across a raging fire, the flames of fear and dread caused by the terrible wither finally extinguished. Slowly, he stood and stared at the demolished tunnel; he'd barely made it out of the Cave of Slumber. If he had been the tiniest bit slower, he'd either be dead or taking an eternal nap.

Thank you, he thought to the Flail. *I couldn't have done it without you.*

Three voices replied in his mind. *We must remain ever watchful; there is still a monster somewhere nearby.*

Watcher glanced around nervously, looking for threats, but surrounding him were friends; there were only villagers in the chamber. They were safe.

"So . . . it's done." There was a finality to Watcher's voice that lifted the spirits of his friends. "We did it."

"We did it!" Cutter boomed. The big NPC grabbed the nearest person and gave them a huge hug. Only after he let go did he realize it was Er-Lan.

The little zombie was surprised, but when Cutter smiled, Er-Lan smiled as well.

Planter wrapped her arms around Watcher, a joyous smile on her square face. She hugged him tight, refusing to let go.

"Planter . . . we need to talk about what happened with the Bow."

"No," she whispered in his ear. "Just wait. Let me enjoy holding you for a minute before everything changes."

And so he waited . . . and waited . . .

"That's the longest victory hug I've ever seen," Blaster said, laughing.

Watcher's cheeks grew hot as he and Planter finally let go of each other.

Blaster started saying something, but Watcher held up a glowing hand, stopping his friend. He turned back to Planter and gazed into her deep emerald eyes.

"Planter, you picked up the Bow of Destruction, knowing it would kill you," Watcher said. "Why?"

A tear tumbled from Planter's eye. "That wither and the zombies were going to destroy you. Its flaming skulls had wounded you, and I knew you'd never be able to stop the zombies before they reached you. I couldn't live without you, so I figured I might as well do something to keep you safe, even if it cost me my life."

"But it didn't."

She shook her head.

"You know what that must mean?"

Planter nodded, an expression of resignation on her beautiful face. "I must be a descendant of some wizard."

"And you have magical powers as well," Watcher added.

Planter nodded again. "You remember this?" She pulled out the Amulet of Planes they'd found in the Wizard's Tower. "I was able to hear it singing to me when nobody else could. I also heard the Gauntlets of Life when they were buried in the Compass. That's when I started to suspect something was wrong."

"Nothing's wrong," Watcher said. "Just because you

have magical powers, it doesn't mean you're flawed or . . ."

"Different? Is that what you're saying? That you and I aren't different from everyone else?"

"Well . . ." Watcher grew quiet, knowing the truth in her words. "We may be different, but at least we're together, right?" He gazed into her eyes. "We *are* together, aren't we?" He stepped closer to her. "Have you forgiven me for being a fool and taking you for granted? I can't guarantee I won't be an idiot again, but I will *never* take you for granted or seek fame again. All I want is to be with you and have everyone safe."

She looked down at his glowing hands, then took them in hers. "I think I can live with that."

A huge smile spread across Watcher's face. It almost made his cheeks hurt. Planter giggled, then hugged him again.

"I think it's time we left this place before we discover any new monsters from the Great War," Mapper said.

"I like that idea," Fencer said. "After all this excitement, I don't think it was such a great choice to follow all of you to this terrifying place."

"Ya think?" Blaster asked.

"Let's get moving. I want to get home," Watcher said as he glanced at Planter and took her hand in his, "and just live in peace."

Planter nodded.

Fencer scowled at him.

They headed for the door, but when they reached the piles of items on the ground, Watcher stopped and stared at them, a sad expression on his face. NPCs had died here fighting Krael and the Broken Eight. Slowly, he raised his hand into the air, fingers spread wide, the other villagers doing the same. Clenching his fist, he squeezed his hand tight.

"I'm sorry I couldn't protect you," he whispered, "but your sacrifices saved the Far Lands, and possibly all of Minecraft."

Watcher squeezed his fist tighter, knuckles popping. A tear tumbled down his cheek, but he didn't wipe it away; he let it fall to the ground. Planter put a hand on his shoulder, then reached up and pulled his hand down. Watcher opened his fist and saw that his fingernails had dug into his glowing palm, leaving deep indentations in his skin.

"It's not your fault," Planter said in a soft, soothing voice.

Watcher said nothing; he just stared at the items for a moment, then knelt and picked them all up. Glancing at his friends, he pointed to the chamber exit. "Let's get out of here."

They moved toward the tunnel with Fencer near the front. Suddenly, an angry moan filled the chamber. The last surviving zombie from the Broken Eight jumped out of the shadows and lunged at Fencer with its sword.

Before anyone could react, a knife tumbled through the air and struck the monster in the chest, the blade sticking into its golden armor. The monster stopped for a moment, smiled, then swung its blade at Fencer. Another knife streaked through the air, but this time, it struck the handle of the blade already sticking out of the zombie's chest and drove the first knife through the armor and into the monster's flesh.

The zombie staggered back, flashing red as it clawed at the blade, but it was beneath the creature's armor. Watcher drew Needle, but suddenly Blaster tore it from his hands and threw it like a spear. The enchanted blade sailed through the air, leaving a line of sparkling particles behind as it hit the zombie in the side, taking the last of the creature's HP. With a sorrowful moan, the last of the Broken Eight disappeared, its armor and weapon fading into nothingness.

"Fencer, are you alright?" Mapper asked.

The girl was still shocked by what had almost happened; she was speechless.

Blaster moved forward and picked up his knives,

then handed Needle back to Watcher. He moved to Fencer and shook her gently by the shoulders.

"Fencer, are you okay?" Blaster asked. "That was close."

The terrified expression on her face slowly faded away as she looked at her savior.

"Blaster, you're the bravest, most important person in all of Minecraft." She smiled a huge, joyous smile. "I'm gonna take care of you . . . forever."

A look of sudden terror spread across Blaster's face. He glanced at Planter and Watcher, eyes wide.

"You're a lucky guy . . . Fencer is gonna take care of you forever." Watcher smiled.

"Yeah," Planter added. "For–ev–er."

Blaster glanced at the other villagers, hoping to find help, but the rest of the NPCs just smiled, enjoying the boy's misery.

"Come on, Blaster." Fencer grabbed his arm with both hands. "Let's walk together as we head home."

She pulled him into the tunnel, a satisfied grin on her face. Blaster glanced over his shoulder at Watcher and mouthed *HELP* to him. Watcher just smiled.

"Come on, everyone," Watcher said. "It's time to head home."

Then, with Planter's hand in his, they walked away from the Cave of Slumber and toward home.

AVAILABLE NOW FROM MARK CHEVERTON AND SKY PONY PRESS

HEROBRINE REBORN SERIES
Gameknight999 and his friends and family face Herobrine in the biggest showdown the Overworld has ever seen!

Gameknight999, a former Minecraft griefer, got a big dose of virtual reality when his father's invention teleported him into the game. Living out a dangerous adventure inside a digital world, he discovered that the Minecraft villagers were alive and needed his help to defeat the infamous virus, Herobrine, a diabolical enemy determined to escape into the real world.

Gameknight thought Herobrine had finally been stopped once and for all. But the virus proves to be even craftier than anyone could imagine, and his XP begins inhabiting new bodies in an effort to escape. The User-that-is-not-a-user will need the help of not only his Minecraft friends, but his own father, Monkeypants271, as well, if he has any hope of destroying the evil Herobrine once and for all.

Saving Crafter (Book One):
$9.99 paperback • 978-1-5107-0014-7

Destruction of the Overworld (Book Two):
$9.99 paperback • 978-1-5107-0015-4

Gameknight999 vs. Herobrine (Book Three):
$9.99 paperback • 978-1-5107-0010-9

AVAILABLE NOW FROM MARK CHEVERTON AND SKY PONY PRESS

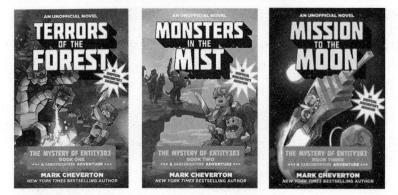

THE MYSTERY OF ENTITY303 SERIES
Minecraft mods are covering the tracks of a mysterious new villain!

Gameknight999 reenters Minecraft to find it completely changed, and his old friends acting differently. The changes are not for the better.

Outside of Crafter's village, a strange user named Entity303 is spotted with Weaver, a young NPC Gameknight knows from Minecraft's past. He realizes that Weaver has somehow been kidnapped, and returning him to the correct time is the only way to fix things.

What's worse: Entity303 has created a strange and bizarre modded version of Minecraft, full of unusual creatures and biomes. Racing through the Twilight Forest and MystCraft, and finally into the far reaches of outer space, Gameknight will face his toughest challenge yet in a Minecraft both alien and dangerous.

Terrors of the Forest (Book One):
$9.99 paperback • 978-1-5107-1886-9

Monsters in the Mist (Book Two):
$9.99 paperback • 978-1-5107-1887-6

Mission to the Moon (Book Three):
$9.99 paperback • 978-1-5107-1888-3

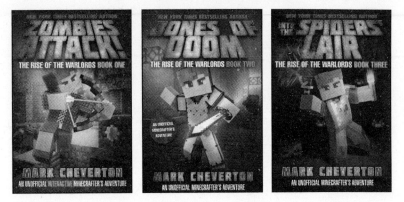

EXCERPT FROM
THE WITHERS AWAKEN
A BRAND NEW FAR LANDS ADVENTURE

The villagers followed Mirthrandos across the landscape, continuing westward. Watcher led the company in a defensive formation as they ran, and the boy worried about any more monstrous surprises coming from the leafy canopy overhead. Fortunately, none of the treetop inhabitants came down to challenge them, though Watcher was able to see shapes moving through the leaves. The monsters were still up there, watching and waiting.

The gigantic trees slowly grew smaller as they traveled through the biome, the forest gradually morphing into something Watcher would expect to see in the Far Lands—a birch forest with a smattering of oaks here and there, colorful splashes of flowers nestled within tall blades of grass. The company darted through the beautiful forest, racing the sun as it slowly descended toward the western horizon.

Watcher assumed they'd have to stop so that Mirthrandos could rest, but the old woman had no problem keeping up with the rest of them. Her immortality apparently kept her fit as well. They ran in silence, each villager listening for the approach of monsters, but the forest was peaceful and calm. The sound of cows, chickens, and pigs floated from between the pristine, white birch trees, but as before, the animals were nowhere in sight.

"You notice it again?" Blaster said to Watcher.

"What?"

"Animal sounds, but no animals." Blaster pulled off his forest green cap to scratch his head. His black curls instantly sprang outward, yearning for freedom, but were quickly captured again by the leather cap.

"Yeah . . . this is strange." Watcher pulled Needle from his inventory as he glanced to the left and right, looking for the animals, but finding none.

"Hey Mirthrandos," Blaster said, moving closer to the old woman. "What was the deal with all the flames on the lake?"

"You liked my flames?" The ancient wizard smiled.

"Well . . . not at first, but it was a neat trick."

"I put those there to keep anyone from bothering me in my underwater home." She glanced at Watcher and glared. "Apparently it didn't work very well."

"You have to try much harder than that to keep Watcher from bugging you." Blaster laughed.

"Apparently so," she said, then laughed with Blaster.

"Mirthrandos, can I ask you a question?" Planter swerved around a birch tree, then moved to the old woman's side.

"Of course, dear."

"You were around during the Great War?"

The old woman nodded. "Bad times, yes it was, very bad times, indeed."

"How is it you're still alive?" Planter asked.

"I was given eternal life from one of our greatest wizards. Tharus was his name; I'm sure you've run across his name in books more than once."

Watcher shrugged, but Mapper moved to the young girl's side and nodded.

"I've read many accounts about Tharus and his incredible powers," Mapper said. "The books say he was powerful, wise, and kind."

The ancient wizard laughed. "One of those three are true."

"You must have done something incredible to be given the gift of eternal life," Watcher said.

"Gift . . . ha!" Mirthrandos scowled. "It was a punishment."

"A punishment?" Watcher didn't understand.

The old woman nodded her head, her gray hair glowing a soft orange as the dusk sun spread its crimson light across the landscape. "Yes, I did something that was unthinkable to the *great wizards*."

"What did you do?" Planter asked.

Mira sighed. "I showed mercy to a monster." She glanced over her shoulder at the other NPCs. "All of you have learned to show mercy to a monster, even when you know what they are." She pointed at Er-Lan with a crooked, wrinkled finger. "You know what he is, yet you allow him to be with your company, in peace."

"I don't know what you mean by *what he is,* but Er-Lan is part of our family," Watcher said.

"Back in my day, that was an unforgivable thing to do." Mirthrandos reached out and put an arm around Watcher's glowing shoulders. "I showed mercy to a young wither who wanted no part in the violence spreading across the land. When Tharus learned what I had done, he punished me by making me the caretaker of Wizard City and the guardian of the Weapons Vault."

"Punishment, I don't understand." Watcher stared into the old woman's bright green eyes. "You can never die . . . how is that a punishment?"

"It is the cruelest and most severe of punishments. Tharus knew exactly what he was doing to me when he cast that spell." An expression of rage spread across Mira's wrinkled face. "He was cruelest of the wizards, though history paints him as a hero."

"I don't understand, Mirthrandos," Watcher said. "Not being able to die seems like a good thing."

"I've been alive for three hundred and seventy-eight years."

"Three hundred and seventy-eight?!" Watcher and Planter said in unison, both shocked.

"Time ticks at a different rate in this world," the ancient wizard said. "Do you know how many husbands and children and grandchildren I've had?"

"Well, I'd guess—"

"I've had to watch every one of them grow old as time ravaged their bodies. I've had to stand there, helpless as they died in my arms, and have grieved for them when their bodies finally disappeared from the surface of Minecraft." Her eyes glowed bright with anger. "I've collected every bit of XP from each one when they passed so that I'd have something of theirs that would survive with me through eternity."

"That's terrible," Watcher said.

"It's so sad," Planter sniffled as a tear leaked from an eye. "That's why you know right where the Weapons Vault is located, right? You're its caretaker."

Mira nodded, her gray hair bobbing up and down.

"I'm sorry." Planter placed a hand on the wizard's shoulder, but she brushed her hand away.

"I don't need your pity," Mirthrandos snapped. "I've lived longer than all you kids put together. I don't need anything from any of you. All I want to do is get you these portal keys so you can get out of my life and leave me in peace."

"But what about the war?" Watcher asked. "Krael has been encouraging monsters to attack villagers all across this land. He has rekindled the Great War."

She stared at him with a blank expression on her wrinkled face.

"And now that the withers have escaped the Cave of Slumber and are free, they'll try to destroy everything," Planter said. "We need your help to stop them."

The wizard laughed. "My part in the Great War is over, Tharus saw to that. I see two wizards before me and others behind you who can help if you know where to look. This is *your* war now. My place is in my underwater home, staring at the squid and fish until time itself finally stops. That's what I have to look forward to; everything else is just a distraction."

An uneasy silence spread across the company as the woman's words, with their vile contempt at just being alive, etched their way into their souls. Watcher knew everyone felt sorry for her, but that was no reason just to give up. He glanced at her; Mirthrandos' eyes already focused on him, boring into his head as if she could read his mind.

Watcher was about to speak when the sounds of arrows zipping through the air filtered through the forest. Instantly, Watcher reached for the Flail of Regrets as Planter drew her red shield emblazoned with three wither heads across the red center, the rest of their companions grabbing their weapons.

"Well, look what we have here!" Mirthrandos knelt before Watcher and stared at the Flail, a huge smile on her face, then laughed. "It's like seeing old friends again. Hello Balltheron, how are you doing in there?"

She smiled, then turned to Planter. The ancient wizard leaned forward as if speaking to her shield. "Good to see you again, Sotaria." She laughed. "Is the tiny grain piece of you in there able to communicate, or did they divide you too many times?"

"What are you talking about?" Watcher asked.

"I knew your friends there before they sent their minds into those weapons," Mirthrandos said. She stared down at the Flail. "You've never looked better, Baltheron."

"You mean there really *is* a wizard in there?" Blaster asked.

The old woman nodded.

"Huh . . . I thought he was just crazy when he was talking to that thing." Blaster smiled.

Watcher frowned. "I heard arrows. There must be skeletons nearby."

"Come . . . follow me." Mirthrandos moved around a clump of bushes, allowing them to see the terrain ahead.

Before them stood a huge valley, with steep mountains on either side, the range extending out to the left and right, impossible to pass. The setting sun cast a crimson hue across the landscape, causing long shadows to stretch out across the ground as if they were reaching toward the intrepid companions. Within the valley, tall columns of dispensers stood at least six high, standing all throughout the terrain, their faces pointing in every direction. Each dispenser spat out arrows, sending a constant storm of pointed shafts all across the landscape.

"Welcome to the Valley of Arrows," Mirthrandos said. "This is the great secret of Tharos. Here lies the hidden Wizard City and within, the Weapons Vault."

"You mean we have to go . . . through the valley to get to the Vault?" Mapper asked, his voice cracking with fear.

The ancient wizard laughed. "We don't go through the Valley of Arrows to get to Wizard City." She shook her head in disbelief. "The great Wizard City is *in* the Valley."

"But I don't see anything other than arrows," Blaster said.

Watcher glanced around. There were a few hills of stone and gravel here and there leading to the Valley of Arrows, but no other features visible.

"Just follow me." Mirthrandos walked toward the edge of the Valley of Arrows, then stepped into it, heedless of the pointed shafts flashing through the air. And in an instant, she was gone . . . disappearing from sight.

"What happened?" Watcher asked.

But before anyone could respond, a harsh laugh filled the air. Tiny square goosebumps formed on Watcher's arms as the cackle filled the air.

"Krael," Blaster hissed. Watcher nodded.

Slowly, the king of the withers, wearing three Crowns of Skulls, slowly rose up from behind a line of trees, his army of dark monsters at his back.

"So I see we meet again, boy," the wither king screeched.

The other withers slowly spread out across the tree-tops, each positioning themselves for a clear line of fire. The villagers slowly backed up, terrified expressions on their square faces. Only Watcher and Planter held their ground.

"I think it is time for you to be deleted from Minecraft. And when we're done with you, we'll destroy your friends." Krael laughed again. "Then, we'll begin the destruction of the Far Lands."

Watcher and Planter took a step backward, then another, both getting ready to turn and run, but then Krael's eyes grew bright with rage. The other withers, seeing this, also prepared their own flaming skulls, their eyes growing bright as well.

"Withers . . . FIRE!"

And hundreds of flaming skulls descended upon Watcher and Planter.

COMING SOON:
THE WITHERS AWAKEN: WITHER WAR BOOK TWO